Bodies & Soul

Bodies & Soul

musical memoirs by

Al Young

creative arts book company
berkeley 1981

For radiant
Andrea
&
for Barry;
with fond
memories
of Mt. Holyoke
&
with
admiration
for your
work; its tender
exactitudes. Love, Al

100

Several of these selections, in somewhat different form, first appeared in *Beloit Poetry Journal, The Black Scholar, Callaloo, City Miner, El Corno Emplumado* (Mexico City), *Parabola,* and *Spero.* "Black Pearls" and "Remembering Pepper Adams and Donald Byrd" were commissioned respectively by Ralph J. Gleason and Orrin Keepnews as liner notes for the Prestige LPs: *Black Pearls* (John Coltrane) and *Young Byrd* (Donald Byrd / Pepper Adams / Gigi Gryce). "Gifts and Messages" was written originally as jacket copy for a Rahsaan Roland Kirk album.

Published by Creative Arts Book Company, 833 Bancroft Way, Berkeley, California 94710. Book Design by George Mattingly, with calligraphy by Sandy Diamond, typography by Sam Doleman, author photo by Lee Marsullo, and cover photo by Kaz Tsuruta, from the book *Jukebox: The Golden Age,* Lancaster-Miller Publishers, Berkeley, CA. Printed in the United States of America. ISBN 0-916870-39-1.

Creative Arts Books are published by Donald S. Ellis.

contents

"All music is what awakens from you
when you are reminded by the instruments."

—Walt Whitman

"I think constantly about the lyrics and what they mean, and I try and make my listeners feel the vision of what the words are saying. All of us know about sorrow and tears and laughter, so it's not my job to sing *my* emotions but to sing my *listeners'* emotions. Then they can take them home with them."

—Mabel Mercer

from Whitney Balliet's
ALEC WILDER AND HIS FRIENDS

"All songs are born in man out in the great wilderness. Without ourselves knowing how it happens, they come with the breath, words and tones that are not daily speech."

—Kilíme

(an Eskimo poet of Hudson Bay
described in Peter Freuchen's *BOOK OF THE ESKIMOS*)

*For Michael who will one day
understand his father's love
of freedom.*

intro

When my father was getting ready to leave this world, I was fortunate to have been on hand, by his bedside mostly, to share the intense pleasure he derived from listening to tape recordings I brought him of the very music on which he had weaned me. "This brings it all back," he said, beaming and positively clear of eye, shrunken though he was from cancer. "Those were the happiest days of my life. I can hear everything. I can see it. I try to keep up, you know, but the stuff they play now—with all that fancy equipment and electricity they got—somehow it just don't sound like music to me."

I was only too happy to be giving back to my father, if only for a fraction of a moment in eternity, some of the lasting magic he lavished on me while I was still a child in Mississippi and Michigan and in no hurry whatever to become an adult. Because of him, I grew up in a house filled with records and with living music. Music was always there with me—at home, on the streets, in church, at school, on the radio, at movies, social gatherings, dances; in concert halls, nightclubs, restaurants, lofts, shacks, mansions, kitchens, backrooms, warehouses, labs, hotel rooms, tents, alleys, elevators, shops, automobiles, on boats; in love, at war, in peace, and even in my sleep. I can still remember as clearly as if it were today the very first music that touched me: early songs that I sang, the first notes I ever sounded on a piano, spacious cricket concertos on summer nights, the tinkle of spoons against cups and water glasses, birdcalls, blues, spirituals, actual hollers in Mississippi fields where I picked my early share of cotton and corn and cut a little cane; my grandmother's voice and her constant humming as she went about her everyday tasks, the melodious rise and fall in the voices of Afro-Christian preachers in little tumble-down country churches, the rapid rat-a-tat of peckerwood percussion, country laments, heavy-duty juke joint fried fish and barbecue funk, jazz in all its endless guises and disguises, the swishing of leaves, the sounds of cities, the hush of streams and the roar of the ocean.

One night in Detroit, where I reached adolescence, I was safe in my room, embarked on a musical voyage that took me from Igor Stravinsky's *Le Sacre du Printemps* to Charlie Parker's "Now's the Time" and the timeless "Koko," his startling mutation of Ray Noble's "Cherokee." I was about to take a breather and play some Muddy Waters to relax when my mother, with a chuckle in her voice, called me downstairs. The weekly Dorsey Brothers show was on, so it must have been early Saturday night.

"I just thought you might like to check this joker out," she said, gesturing toward the TV screen that held her spellbound.

There, glowing and gyrating in the half-light of our living room, was Elvis Presley—sideburns, bright suit, black shirt, open collar and guitar—doing what can only be described as a slightly uncool bump and grind while he growled out Little Richard's smash hit, "Tutti Fruti," the follow-up to his outrageous "Long Tall Sally."

"Well," said my mother, "I don't think I've ever seen a white boy could cut up like that. Betcha anything he'll make a fortune."

"Why do you say that?"

"Because he's doing our stuff, but he isn't one of us. They're crazy about our style, but they don't care much for us. As a Negro man with some talent and intelligence you won't have an easy time of it. You'll find out what I mean just as sure as you're born."

If, from the time I was born to the days of my departure, I could assemble and sample all of the music that has affected my life—the sublime, the bewitching, the entertaining, the adequate, the functional, the tedious and the forgettable—I know that it would be the perfect way to re-live this fleet, uncertain residence on Earth. Music has a way of evoking past moments and entire eras, if not lifetimes, that is immutably unique. While drowning in a sea of sound, my whole life passes before me.

But everything moves on and gets changed around. Charlie Parker, it's said, died strangely in the apartment of a baroness in New York while laughing at some jugglers on the Dorsey Brothers TV Show. Bird, as Parker was nicknamed, claimed that Jimmy Dorsey was one of his all-time favorite saxophonists. Elvis did go on to make more than one fortune. White people took over rock and roll. My mother was right about that too, but even Elvis died under mysterious circumstances a few years after I had the good luck of witnessing

Stravinsky take a somewhat creaky, smiling bow from the first row balcony of U.C. Berkeley's Zellerbach Auditorium following a scintillating staging of his ballet, *L'Histoire du Soldat*, one of my all-time favorites, with Gregory Peck as narrator.

Simultaneity has always enthralled me: the ways in which human suffering and joy are endlessly connected. Time and timelessness, soul and spirituality, the physical universe crammed with celestial bodies as the natural extension, in both space and mind, of our own fragile, terrestrial organisms—this is what continues to warm, nurture and strengthen me in my eternal flight into light. And it is music that helps organize my feelings and thoughts, reminding me that none of us is ever truly alone, for when we interact with music, either in solitude or in gatherings, small or large, what are we listening for but the human spirit sung or played or catching its breath in an invisible world where sound is to silence as day is to night?

Little did I know when I began this book that I would be opening up within myself a region so vast that it could never be fully explored or charted, and certainly not within the breadth and boundaries of a single volume. My only wish for these tender pages of solos, takes and breaks—call them prose-poems, essays, stories, memoirs, sketches, whatever you fancy—is that they will give as much pleasure to readers and listeners all over the world as life—for all its pain and uncertainty—has given me.

If I stray a bit from the melody at times and vary the beat, it's because I'm learning what you already know so well about the meaning and sense of it all. The song, indeed, has always been you, and it will forever be turning back into itself.

Al Young
Perth, Western Australia
and Singapore
Summer 1981

Bodies & Soul

body and soul

COLEMAN HAWKINS, 1939

My father, who used to bicycle thirty miles one way to court
my mother, had this record among his dust-needled 78s. He'd
already worn out several copies before I learned to love it
from memory, never knowing until much later what a cause
it had stirred.

Imagine it's 1939. You talk about a hellraising year, that
one had to take the cake with Hitler taking Czechoslovakia,
Bohemia, Moravia and Poland; with Stalin taking Finland and

Poland (poor Poland); Franco taking Spain; Great Britain and France declaring war on Germany; Mussolini taking Albania; Stalin and Hitler signing their infamous non-aggression pact that would splinter and split all the left-leaning parents of kids I would later meet at college and beyond. My own folks, peasants and proles, knew next to nothing about the left-wing or right-wing of anything but chickens, but they did know right from wrong. Politics to them had something to do with money and power, which in white Mississippi were one and the same.

History and truth are so easily misconstrued. Even dates, names, facts and figures can lie—"Aught's an aught / Figger's a figger / All for the white man / None for the nigger"—depending on who's doing the dating, doing the naming, doing the figuring. The telling of truth is the poet's proper domain and in the head-whipping nations of this darkening, fact-ridden world, people still look to poets and the music they make for light, sweet light illumining everything everywhere.

If it's true that in this alleged 1939 the New York World's Fair "World of Tomorrow" ran for five straight months and that TVA got the Supreme Court go-ahead and that TV in the U.S. was first broadcast publicly from the Empire State Building (covering the opening of that same World's Fair), then it's equally fair to imagine Coleman Hawkins in that crowded year. In October, the Golden Gate Bridge closed down for repairs while on the eleventh day of that same month, Hawkins, just back from a rewarding stay in war-hungry Europe, repaired to the RCA Victor New York studios with some musical friends and cut "Body and Soul"—just like that, in the shadow of the Empire State Building.

You can even picture him slouched in front of one of those weighty old condenser boom mikes, surrounded by smoke, suspendered and hatted, thinking something like: "Well, let's see how what I'm feeling's gonna come out sounding this time, so we can get this session wrapped up and get back to the gig and really do some blowing." After the take he probably remembered how he'd performed this wee hours ballad better a hundred times before. "I'll get it down yet," he told himself, "but this'll have to do for now." And, children, that was that.

When the record came out, saxophonists all over the world, hearing it and sensing that things would never be the same, started woodshedding Hawkins' impassioned licks in their closets and on the stand. Why'd he have to go and do that? Of course, everybody fell in love with it. My father would play it, take it off, play something else, then put it back on. This went on for years. What was he listening for? What were we listening to? What did it mean? What were all those funny, throaty squawks and sighs and cries all about? I knew what a body was, but what was a soul? You kept hearing people say, "Well, bless his soul!" You thought you knew what they meant, but really, you could only imagine as you must now. You knew what they meant when they said "Bless her heart!" because you could put your hand to your heart and feel the beat, and your Aunt Ethel sometimes fried up chicken hearts along with gizzards, livers and feet. But a soul was unseeable. Did animals have souls too? Did birds, dogs, cows, mules, pigs, snakes, bees? And what about other stuff, like corn, okra, creeks, rivers, moonlight, sunshine, trees, the ground, the rain, the sky? Did white folks have souls?

Was a soul something like a breeze: something you couldn't picture or grab but could only feel like you could the wind off the Gulf when the day cooled down, or the way the ground would tremble when the train roared past across the street from where we lived?

Thirty-nine, forty, fifty, a hundred, thousands—who's to say how many rosy chilled Octobers have befallen us, each one engraved in micro-moments of this innocent utterance, electrically notated, but, like light in a photograph, never quite captured in detail, only in essence. Essence in this instance is private song, is you hearing your secret sorrow and joy blown back through Coleman Hawkins, invisibly connected to you and played back through countless bodies, each one an embodiment of the same soul force.

All poetry is about silent music, invisible art and the clothing of time for the ages.

cocktails for two

SPIKE JONES & HIS CITY SLICKERS, 1946

"It's a fact," Bookus told me that night as he stared through the windshield at the foggy highway ahead and sucked on the butt of a Camel. "When I was a kid I was crazy about bull-shit—Fatty Arbuckle, Andy Gump, Bob Steele, Butterbeans and Suzie, Stepin Fetchit, Tarzan, Krazy Kat and all like that. You too young to know about it, but we couldn't get enough of that stuff, the same as you can't get enough of this Spike Jones."

Our destination: Chicago. That's right—Chicago Ella Noise, as Bookus called it. My mother, for some forgotten reason, had packed my toothbrush, a sweater, some underwear, pajamas, fresh britches and funnybooks and turned me loose with Bookus McGee. With his razorline mustache, Army issue slacks, scuffed brown zip-up leather jacket and greasy broadbrimmed hat, Bookus looked pretty much like the colored version of every second-string villain you've ever beheld in a 1940s B movie, except we didn't rate them that way then; to us they were all just pictures.

Picture us hunched up in that all but rusted out humpback V-8 Ford with the radio playing more static than fade. What Bookus was doing was hauling a load of bootleg whiskey he had distilled and bottled himself, hauling it across southern Michigan to northern Illinois. If any cop had stopped us, it would've been curtains for Bookus, and no telling what might've happened to me. Naturally, I didn't know that then. All I knew was we were on a weekend trip to visit an old buddy of his who owned a gas station way out in the Land of California, Sweet Home Chicago. Chicago. As in boom-chicka / boom-chicka / Chi / Ca / Go.

And go we did. Chugging us along, cargo and all, was Bookus with his Camels, Bookus with his Spearmint gum, Bookus with his toothpicks, Bookus with his facial scars from a car crash of years ago that had gotten him off hooch (his own and anybody else's) except to sell. There was also Bookus who used to sing blues and play the guitar, Bookus with his Army stories, and Bookus with his dreams.

"Yeah," he kept saying, "all kids love bullshit."

And it was true, for I loved Bookus with his scary tales of what had gone on before I was born, and his way of selling futures tickled me.

"We git to my buddy's gas station," he winked, "and you can drink all the sodapop your belly can hold and don't even have to pay."

And that was true too. All next day I soaked up Pepsis,

Nehis and 7-Ups while they did their grown folks' talk and leaned on cars and crawled under them. That night I peed the bed something awful and got up wanting to hide on Mars.

"Well," said Bookus, "look like we gon' have to tie a little milk bottle around your weenie when you get put to bed."

We laughed at that, but I was looking at it literally and thinking about how I might have to sleep sitting up all night.

The moment I hear "Cocktails for Two" with all those razzes and clinks and horns going "Ooooga-Ooooga!" I fall back into the back seat of that car to grab a nap and look at how it all started out for me, a curious little sub-American boy recalling with perfect clarity the sound of Bookus' Mississippi voice saying, "That's right, it use to be all kids loved bullshit. Now, commence to find out, grown people like it too. That's all you git nowdays is more and more bullshit. You mark my words, the day's comin when bullshit will rule this very world."

fingertips (part 2)

STEVIE WONDER, 1963

That was a year I'm still working with. My days and nights ran all the way from prehistoric times to right now, backward and forward, with God's eyes shining out of skies while I stayed up and up for days on joy. I zipped around cities and towns, flew to the sun, shivered and shouted, dragged beer cartons and shoppingbags full of hot papered ideas from coast to coast, and peed love.

Sometimes when Tom Heineman would be upstairs practicing Mozart sonatas on his mellowing cello, I'd be right there under him in my student-style digs, plucking out hand-woven nitwit music on a borrowed guitar. That was the same spring that (Little) Stevie Wonder started spreading his happiness all over the place.

The first time I caught it was on bassist Tom Glass' car radio. What a jolt that was! It followed us all the way to Sierra Sound Studios in South Berkeley where we were headed to make a record produced by Chris "Arhoolie" Strachwitz, the man who gave the world so many beautiful Mance Lipscombs. At the time Chris was seriously toying with the idea of putting out a 45rpm single of me, by then the most reluctant of folksingers. For two Saturdays in a row, we sweated miking, technical problems and intrusions by an engineer who didn't seem to like people. We worked our butts off on renditions of "San Francisco Bay Blues," Jesse Fuller's tune, and the classic "Baby, Please Don't Go." Bluesman K. C. Douglas, who's dead now, even turned up at the session in his city worker overalls and San Francisco Giants baseball cap to lend support, white-haired and encouraging as he loomed in the background. Still, it just didn't work out. The record never happened. Luck, as it turned out, was with us.

But Stevie's hit took off and followed me all across the country. In Motown that same year I witnessed a crumbling Detroit noisily poised at the beginning of its end: a preview of the condition that would later turn malignant. When he sang, *"Clap your hands / just a little bit louder / Clap your hands / just a little bit louder!"* Stevie could just as easily have been talking about the fall of the Arsenal of Democracy (Detroit's old nickname from the War) as he was the heated performance at hand.

New York after that was more than just a permissible dream: it was proof that pets, cockroaches and pigeons have New Yorks, just as chopped chicken liver lovers have their New Yorks, and derelicts and Fifth Avenuers and even a visiting Californian such as my old flaming self, infected with

Stevie and wanderlust, could still pony up a stack of shining New Yorks.

"Fingertips" trailed me everywhere that year, right onto the boat bound for Portugal, which disembarked toward the end of that summer from Brooklyn, with its proud Jews, Italians and Negroes (soon to become known again as Blacks) where poet Matt Kahn's grandmother, warm of eye and crusty of voice, said to me: "Europe? Why in the world would you want to go there? It's nothing. I know. I came from there."

Stevie's music comforted me all across the ocean. Somehow it seems to have always been waiting in the offing, blind and crouched, like its creator, to sniff and sound us all out *"Just a little bit of sooo-uuu-woull-woulll!"*

sweet lorraine

NAT KING COLE, 1943

When Nat sang that line about how each night he prayed that no one would steal her heart away, my brothers' ears and mine picked the line up as "Each night I pray / that no one will steal / her hot away."

Her hot away. Now that meant something to three Southern-nurtured tots suddenly brought north where, for that first frozen winter, we were forbidden to venture outside. Can you imagine how frightened our mother must have been for us?

It was a normal situation. Dad had just come back from
Navy duty and this was heaven on the second floor of our
aunt's and uncle-in-law's phony-bricked home. It was Aunt
Ethel who finally told us one warm late March afternoon,
when our mother wasn't around, that we could go outside and
play in the backyard. And what a spring we stepped out into!
There were ants, sowbugs, cocoons—*kacoombs* to us—under
logs. And you should've seen the butterflies! We headed directly for the cherry tree to do some climbing. We've been
climbing ever since, although not so much straight up as out
and around and down into the world.

Nat Cole's world was the sound of warmth. His heated
whisper melted hearts. We'd fooled around up there in the
house long enough to love his voice, which, like the voices of
most hit singers, sounded instantly familiar. It was as if it had
always been there, nibbling at the edges of our earlobes.

We didn't know who Lorraine was and we didn't care.
The fact that she was sweet was good enough. Hot was all we
wanted to be. Sure, we understood that part of the lyric that
dealt with when it was raining and the sunshine being there
in her eyes. But the feeling of the record, as we grew to kind of
love it, was so smooth that it was a little like being dunked
into a warm bath of inexplicable sound.

"*Choo-choo-choy,*" he sang, meaning *choo-choo-toy.*

Hey, we were right there, digging on Nat King Cole who,
as far as we were concerned, was as much a part of our lives
as the faithful baloney sandwiches Mother Dear fixed for
Daddy to take to work at the Chevy plant, or the times they
would get into physical, knife-brandishing fights, or the very
way that things, when you're a kid, go crazy and fester inside
your impressionable head for years on end.

Eventually we each dispersed to find our own special joy
in a cold and hateful, gold-plated world where happiness is
becoming a corny concept tolerated mostly in comic strips
and greeting cards.

only the lonely

FRANK SINATRA, 1958

O let me tell you, you could get dangerously sentimental and deep down into that dark mushiness that saturates the soul past one in the morning when the party isn't over but should be. It was Irish-born poet James McAuley who first sprang that phrase "dark mushiness" on me, over beers at country singer Faron Young's Nashville nightclub years ago. McAuley used it to describe the feeling that comes over gatherers back home in Dublin pubs when the hour is late and singing begins. Eggplant mushiness might be more suitable for my purpose, perhaps to better evoke the color of severely dimmed off-hour party light, or perhaps to best indicate the tipsy capacity that frolicking, late-staying party guests have for absorbing foolishness and self-pity, just as an eggplant can almost endlessly absorb oils and fats.

Looking back, I can easily see how *Only the Lonely* was, in its quiet way, a kind of torchy pop erotica. Emotionally, the album was also equivalent to the mood induced by Fred Astaire in a bar scene from the 1943 movie musical, *The Sky's the Limit*, where he's the only drunk left at the bar. Decked out tastefully, as always, Astaire closes the joint spectacularly by turning to the straight-man bartender and addressing him in song as he moodily intones "One For My Baby (And One More for the Road)."

You may not know it either, but I too am a kind of a poet who's got a lot of things to say about how someone would inevitably drag out this evergreen LP at the butt end of a party. The album itself, with its *hotel moderne* jacket illustration, depicted Sinatra as a Laugh-Sad-Clown Pagliacci with reddened bittersweet teardrops slipping from his Modigliani greasepaint eyes. And the rightness of his crooning against a mutely fiddled background, cutting through the smoke of a room that had begun to fill on Saturday night and in which you'd languished until Sunday before dawn—well, that sound was all you needed to hear to know that this might very well be your last chance to do some woozy, slow-motion stumbling and fumbling around the dance floor.

It was at such a Berkeley party in the very early sixties that I heard longshoreman intellectual Jimmy Lynn tell some boogie-happy guest of his: "Hey, man, be quiet and let the paddy boy sing! White folks got a right to sing too, you know."

Thus was the mutually solitary mood contained and maintained. Responding to inner alarms, we all slid slowly down that well-greased pole of self-pity and raced with muffled sirens directly to where the fire was.

Fire, schmire! Desire was what it was all about, or, more properly, longing—a longing so vague and at the same time so vast and unquenchable that it still would've been pointless for either you or your momentary partner to shed your clothes and offer your quivering bodies, wet or erect, to one another right there on the spot in the middle of "Willow Weep for Me."

backwater blues

BESSIE SMITH, 1927

Bessie's got her flood and I've got mine. Mine was 1947, the year I lived with my Aunt Doris and Uncle Cleve and their kids, my cousins Mary, Martha and Ray in Laurel, Mississippi.

It rained and rained for days and days. In that Southern Baptist household, we took the Old Testament—and the New Testament, for that matter—literally. "God gettin ready to claim His own," Aunt Lou kept telling us—Aunt Lou, my uncle's strangely sanctified sister who went around habitually in a blueberry-colored nun's outfit of her own design.

Finally it looked as if her words were coming true when the creek water rose so high that my cousin Ray and I came out one morning to see the front steps submerged. Aw, it was something! We kids, of course, were all pulling for the flood since it meant we wouldn't have to go to school. "Just stay home and play and have fun and stuff," I told Cousin Ray. He had to admit it was great all right, "but what if we all get drownded?" Somehow I knew that wasn't going to happen.

Schedules collapsed. A local state of emergency was declared. Just like in the song, my Uncle Cleve, wearing hip boots and a raincoat, rowed a little boat up to the front door late one dark afternoon and, hallelujah, lowered us down into it one by one. Were we overjoyed? Is water wet? Do boats float? What do kids know or care about furniture and rugs getting ruined or building foundations getting water-logged? Our ace was adventure.

We rowed up and docked on dry land at the house of some family friends who had plenty of kids for us to play with. In no time we became acquainted with their brand of family nonsense and their outlandish ways.

That was just the point. We were all in the world in our own particular ways, and the world was a play place the size of any universe. The world just then was Mississippi with its chinaberry trees and mud, with old rusty roller-skates and medicine bottles bubbling up out of what we hoped wasn't polio water. We didn't pay any more attention to grown folks than they paid to us.

Birds still flew. Flies landed. We bit into pomegranates (*pummagranites,* we called 'em) right off trees. We played ball, rolled tires, acted out dreams and wrestled. I gave my Cousin Ray, the household bully, a fair and square whipping he never forgot. Uncle Cleve kept playing that record he loved called "Little Joe from Chicago" that had a Louis Jordan bounce to it. My aunt and the other women sighed in kitchens where they

made fires, washed greens, snapped beans and fixed neckbones and rice while telling their stories in verbal jam sessions that stopped but never ended.

There we all were, heroes in a story about a flood that
few people knew about, in a place that few people cared about
or even knew existed.

remembering pepper adams & donald byrd

THE WORLD STAGE (DETROIT), *CIRCA* 1955

In those days, a distant version of now, a lot of beautiful music went unrecorded. It sailed out of windows and doorways, escaping into the trees. Much of it got blown up into slowpoke clouds where, liquefied, it fell back to earth; sometimes thunderously, in the form of cleansing rain, or as slow delicious snow.

That was how it felt anyway. The 1950s were fertile, precious years for this ever-changing sound that we're fond of labeling jazz. In Detroit alone there was so much real music afloat that people, mostly without even knowing it, walked and talked and thought and fought to it. Smoky-throated kids on playgrounds and streetcorners harmonized in counterpoint and weren't even studying about cutting a demo or getting discovered. Even the eternal hum of auto traffic flowed and screeched to beats and off-beats.

Picture yourself an energetic 10th grader—dumb, disturbed, inspired—macking, as that indescribable hip walk was called, with a couple of LPs and 45s under one arm, east-siding it across Woodward Avenue, over near Northern High School, when all of a sudden—*doo-weee / bop / oolya-bobba-zweebie-doo-wahhh!*—you'd hear the ring of a solitary trumpet smearing blues all over a sequence of diminished and augmented 7th, 9th and 13th chords. Sweating, frozen in your tracks, you'd stop and look around to see where all those disembodied, weather-changing tones were coming from, and that's when you'd realize you were standing in front of Donald Byrd's family home.

For underage jazz lovers, Sunday afternoons and Monday nights were special. There was no way you were going to fake out the doormen at Baker's Keyboard Lounge, the Flame Show Bar, the West Inn, the Paradise Club, the Chesterfield Lounge, or Club 12, no matter how maturely you decked yourself out or how artfully you colored in your mustache. But you always felt right at home at World Stage, where Sunday afternoons and Monday nights the New Music Society, funded largely by subscribing members, put on concerts in a warmly packed upstairs theater-in-the-round setting.

Looking back, you could say that World Stage was a sort of precursor of the jazz loft. There were no refreshments or floor cushions, but for under a buck fifty—chump change by today's standards—you could fall up and kick back in one of those vintage canvas folding chairs and be transported for hours by the likes of Yusef Lateef, Barry Harris, Louis Hayes, Tommy Flanagan, Thad and Elvin Jones, Harold and Bernard

McKinney, Curtis Fuller, Ernie Farrow, Alice (pre-Coltrane) McLeod, Ernie Wilkins' big band, Lonnie Hilliard, Charles McPherson, Sonny Red, Kenny Burrell, Billy Mitchell, Frank Foster, Tate Houston, Earl Williams, Paul Chambers, Joe Henderson, Dorothy Ashby, Roy Brooks, and on and on.

Musicians were still sitting in and jamming with one another. Veterans and fledglings commingled. You never knew who might be putting in a guest appearance—Sonny Stitt, Art Blakey, Horace Silver, Chet Baker, Carmen McRae, Eddie "Lockjaw" Davis, Terry Gibbs, Cannonball and Nat Adderley, Clifford Brown, Max Roach, Phineas Newborn Jr., Miles Davis.... By the same token, you also had no way of knowing which homegrown notables would next be lured to New York. In its not-so-quiet way, World Stage was a monster!

Two of the most popular hornmen appearing regularly at those World Stage sessions were Donald Byrd and Pepper Adams. As was the case with other locally-based favorites, these shining young instrumentalists were loved and revered for the music they made. Now to understand what that meant in the mid-1950s, you've got to keep in mind that the kinds of extra-musical props and agitprop that music fans later came to take for granted—funny hats and costumes, catchy band names, messianic posturing and weirder-than-thou antics, electronic gimmickry and no-fault fusion / disco / funk— held little or no sway over listening or dancing audiences then.

Like today's authentic gospel or blues, any jazz worthy of the name was expected to be *about* something. The main idea was still to venture out there and play what you had to say meaningfully, with as much feeling and personal inventiveness as you needed to get your story across to those with whom you were communing. It was a two-way avenue of expression along which player and hearer drove and refueled one another and yet, at heart, were one.

There you were on the stand, playing and working at the same time, tickling more than just the ears in the room with your homespun, exuberant, broken-hearted, hurt and happy anecdotes about love and pain and living. And there you also sat, stood or leaned, with undone homework, taking in what you needed, translating what you could hear into vivid gut-level images that lent meaning to your own experience and dreams; responding bodily with rhythmic nods, taps, claps, steps, sways, laughter, and with half-sung cries and inelegant asides. For the moment you were simultaneously both out there and in there, a little like God, doing everything at once. Not only did you get to compose the score and play all the parts; you also got to do the unwriting, changing everything around on the spot, if necessary, plus you had a ringside seat. Now what could be more fun than that?

The key word was *fun*. Pepper Adams, for example, was fun to listen to and watch. So was Donald Byrd, though for totally different reasons. To begin with, Pepper had a way of turning heads at those predominantly Black gatherings. A quiet man, mild of manner, and as self-effacing as he was lanky, he wore his hair in the youthful crewcut style of the Eisenhower Era. Retiring in his Ivy League togs and horn-rimmed glasses, complete with Clark's desert boot loafers, you could've easily pegged him as president of the Wayne State U. Young Republicans, which he wasn't, or as a daytime insurance office worker—which, in fact, he was for a spell—but once he got that baritone saxophone mouthpiece to his lips, there was no mistaking him for anything other than a confirmed creative musician who took his calling seriously. What you remembered afterward was the warmth and pas-sion he breathed into his solos. You came away with the feel-ing that he loved his chosen music enough to have taken pains to absorb the depth of its history.

From your own school band experience you knew that—as a lead instrument—baritone saxophone was anything but easy to master. Traditionally it has been a rhythmic bottom-izing voice in jazz, woodwind cousin to the tuba and string bass. Its solo status was lovingly established by the late Harry

Carney, that indispensable Ellingtonian pioneer, who painted
signs in neon for lads like Leo Parker, Serge Chaloff, Gerry
Mulligan, Lars Gullin, Cecil Payne, Pepper Adams and Nick
Brignola to follow. There were plenty of baritone saxists
around who copped out by limiting themselves to sounding
those showy guttural burps in the basement register that can
have the same aphrodisiac effect on a crowd as a flashy trumpeter whose big stunt is to keep hitting C above high C. As
for Pepper, he seems to have always played the whole horn
with earthy eloquence and wit. His sound to this day is colored by a sense of longing that has deepened with the years.

You also knew you'd never forget the night that Donald
Byrd—home on leave from glittering Manhattan, where along
with Paul Chambers and Jackie McLean, he'd been working
and recording with pianist George Wallington's Quintet at
Cafe Bohemia—led a steaming baker's dozen assortment of
World Stage heavies that included Lateef and Curtis Fuller in
an epic version of bebop Bud Powell's "Parisian Thoroughfare." Because musicians always scrambled to sit in on this
showpiece, a house favorite just then, the thoroughfare was
jammed.

What was unforgettable about that particular performance—recorded, like so many others, only in precious memory—was Byrd's inspired contribution to it. The format, a
loose head arrangement, called for a brisk 2/4 piano vamp
intro that evoked Gershwin's "An American in Paris" beginning. Playing against this, freely and collectively, each performing artist took delight in sketching tonal impressions of
what he imagined to be a Paris boulevard scene. In play-
ful mimicry of traffic hubbub, horns beeped, honked and
squawked, as drivers cruised, shifted gears or came to sudden
glissando halts. While a saxophone siren wailed in the distance, the bass, played arco, made lively sidewalk cafe chit-
chat with a hit-and-run drummer on the move.

In the midst of all this theatrical mood-setting cacoph-
ony, you could clearly make out Byrd's mellifluous brass-

chimed tones; a tender ripe sound you could practically reach up and touch as it glided overhead like some luminous songbird circling the Champs Elysées. Aloft and soaring, bulging with humor, Byrd even dipped down into his crystalline conservatory bag, picking up just enough morsels of *Petrouchka* and *The Soldier's Tale*—pulling a Stravinsky in reverse—to round out the suspenseful effect.

By the time the band had stepped back into 4/4 time and stated Bud's theme, you were still hanging on with a lump in your throat, flying home blind in a taxi, airborne.

You loved the music these people made for the happiness and strength it gave you. Your feelings about them were such that once they made their inevitable moves from Detroit to New York—as Pepper and Byrd had to do—they virtually left holes in your life; deep holes that would later be only partially refilled with recordings and the satisfaction of knowing that they were every bit as beautiful and capable of being widely appreciated as your childlike heart had led you to believe.

pennies
from heaven

FRANK ROSOLINO , 1959

Long before he joined the Stan Kenton band and became famous worldwide, trombonist Frank Rosolino was a flashy, ebullient Motor City Italian born with bebop in his soul. His old boss Stan Kenton once publicly described Rosolino as "a man of few if any quiet moody moments," and that was just how it seemed and sounded when he'd take to the bandstand and heft that tailgate horn of his. The music he made was happy and uplifting, and whenever he opened his mouth to speak or sing, the mood he created was inevitably upbeat and joyful.

Like any good jazz singer worthy of the name, Rosolino took casual liberties with the melody or words of any piece he thought enough of to perform. Without seriously altering the shape or beauty of a song, he was able to make it his own, emotionally and idiomatically, often by slyly personalizing its lyrics. "Everytime it rains, it rains," he used to proclaim, "matzohs and meatballs!" Or, "Everytime it rains, it rains— pretty little white girls!"

That last one used to break them up when he was working Klein's Show Bar, later to become Club 12, at the corner of Pingree and 12th Street in Detroit, right up the street from 1632 Pingree where I lived just before the family moved further north, a mile away, to Edison and 12th. This was the early 1950s, which would put me in Hutchins Junior High, barely into my teens, and so godawful hip and spoiling to be sainted that it must have been all my parents and teachers could do to stand being in the same room with me. There was very little that got past me and my pals. I mean, we knew we'd been dealt a cruel fate by not having been brought up in New York. That kept us from being The Cat's Meow. But at least, considering the sphere we moved in (a kind of pre-pubescent, highly charged stratosphere, really), nobody could say we weren't the Mosquito's Knees, and did we ever buzz! When we heard Charlie Parker and Miles Davis doing "Buzzy," we just took it for granted that they must've been speaking directly to us.

And Frank Rosolino wasn't really talking to nobody but me, poised out there on the nighttime sidewalk in front of Klein's where the aroma of barbecued ribs, fried shrimp and corned beef blended, stalemated, in a neighborhood that was shifting full-tilt from Jewish to Black. Most of the Jewish kids were retreating to Dexter or further northwest, eventually to end up in places like Oak Park. My Uncle James—ever the nimble-tongued operator, who loved the Jews—said, "After the white folks get tired of a neighborhood, they start moving out and sell it to the Jews, then when the Jews get through running it into the ground, they let the Negroes move in, and after that, looks like, it's only the real poor Negroes left to take over."

Frank Rosolino was one of those Black Bottom Sicilians from the Far Eastside who, if I remember correctly, came out of Miller High, as notorious a public school as they allowed in that day. You always heard about students packing guns and switchblades and giving teachers hell at Miller long before *Blackboard Jungle* (with a soundtrack by Bill Haley and the Comets) came out and made all that into a poisonous cliché. Culturally, Rosolino seemed to owe more to Black urban heritage than to his Sicilian ancestors—not that the two traditions were ever mutually exclusive. Jazz impresario Norman Granz, for one, always maintained that the basic audience for his Jazz at the Philharmonic concerts were young Blacks, young Jews and young Italians. Let the sociologists and ethno-musicologists quibble and quarrel over that one.

My point is that Frank Rosolino, from my Detroit on down through my California days, had always struck me as being one of the happiest, most even-tempered men I'd ever seen. A sharp dresser and ever the raffish, bebop Pagliacci, he cut an attractive figure.

In the early 1960s in Oakland, California, Rosolino turned up at a curious little club called the Gold Nugget which appears to have been owned by a Stan Kenton acolyte who regularly brought first-rate former Kenton sidemen up from L.A. to work for a weekend in a small combo setting, or to work as featured soloist with Johnny Coppola's big band. The Sunday night that Rosolino was guesting, I dropped by the Nugget, feeling highly conspicuous as the only Black person in the crowd. Between sets, I got to speak with Rosolino, who insisted that I call him Frank. I told him about the old days when I used to hang around outside Klein's as a kid to catch him.

Frank rolled his big brown eyes, plucked at his dark operatic mustache and, leaning forward, told me in a low voice, "Hey, Blood, I hope you ain't been runnin around tellin everybody about that, 'cause, see, back here over the last few years I been tryin my damndest to pass!"

He did all right for himself too, passing through this world, making people feel good, getting steady work as a much-sought-after recording and TV studio musician. In recent years he had worked with Benny Carter and Maria Muldaur, toured Europe and Japan, was featured soloist on the Merv Griffin Show and had cut any number of memorable albums.

In the summer of 1979 word reached me that Frank Rosolino had shot his wife dead in their Southern California home, then shot both of their sons before turning the gun on himself and blowing his own brains out.

What went wrong? What was the matter? I've since heard explanations, and yet, given the self-portrait the man painted in sound, none of them truly make sense.

You never quite know what kind of pain anyone is suffering from when they pass through your life, smiling and wishing you well, yet leaving entire fields of themselves closed to you as if they sensed the explosive kinds of mines that might lay hidden there. What can I say? Frank won the war most artists must wage against time and the times to go on creating and growing. He'd won the war, but lost some battle we'll never know about. Somewhere along the way, that very rain he played in so dauntlessly must have given way to a raging, private storm that demolished his umbrella and blew his whole house away.

cucurrucucu paloma

EL TRIO LOS PANCHOS, 1962

Everything was all rainbowed up. Even the Orange Crush I was sipping didn't seem quite real. The pastel light of Mexico can strike you that way.

A fly floated right down to my damp nose before changing its mind about making a buzz landing.

So this was Los Mochis, a tiny town in northern Mexico; a rest stop on the bus run from Tijuana to Guadalajara. Guidebooks had taught me that Los Mochis meant The Flies.

Still curious, I had gotten it into my sweating head to check out the regional history and mythology of this place the very next time I visited a library.

It was steamy August in Los Mochis. The antique jukebox glowed and flashed as it sagged in one corner under the heaviness of *guitarras, guitarrones,* Spanishy sighs and Mexican *ayyys* and that singular languor that lingers between the lines of Mexican ballads and *huapangos.* F. Scott Fitzgerald had been on the right track when he wrote, "The train slowed with midsummer languor."

It was the twilight hour when all the noisy men were heatedly cooling themselves over beers, tequilas and rotgut pulques in the swinging-doored cantinas. Women and children and quieter men languished in the zócalo beneath Pepsi legends, speaking Spanish so drowsily that even I, a vacationing fool in his moneyless youth, could understand most of their talk without straining too hard.

While waiting for my *pollo* and *frijoles* (chicken and beans) at the bus station snack counter, I pressed the iced sodapop bottle to my forehead and slid it down around my lowered eyes and cheeks, savoring the cool, momentary contact. I had been dead asleep when the bus pulled into town. Now, ritually aroused, I began to look around and listen closely to where I was.

That's when I became aware of the Trio Los Panchos on the jukebox. *"Cucurrucucu, cantaba,"* they crooned, and *"Cucurrucucu, no llores."* As the music grew on me, I realized how much the words dealt with love in the here and now. That was, after all, where love lived, wasn't it? At the same time I was noticing how I had constantly been fanning flies from the moment I'd set foot in Los Mochis. The pesky things were everywhere! Glancing around, I observed that everyone else was too busy shooing their own flies to pay much attention to mine.

When a flat-faced Indian—El Chato, they might call him—with a Cantinflas mustache walked in workshirted, trailed by what had to be a hefty percentage of the town's fly population, I could no longer contain myself. I doubled over, rested my head on the counter and began to laugh out loud, too loudly.

The whole joint grew silent as everybody turned to stare. It just so happened that I'd also knocked my drink over. One side of my face was soon resting in a bubbly pool of *Oranch Croosh.*

Even as the paunchy counterman was shrugging and winking at the gawking crowd and shaping tiny circles at his graying temples with his index finger, I found myself enjoying every moment of the spectacle I was making.

Watching him drag out his counter-wiping rag, I sat up wondering if I would ever be able to describe the satisfaction it gave me to never have to look up the history of Los Mochis.

what'd I say

RAY CHARLES *LIVE*, 1971

It's June of 1971 and, in the excitement of coaching an exceptionally good take at a recording session, Ray Charles has forgotten where he's left his coffee cup. We all start looking for it—Dave Braithwaite, the chief engineer; Tony Perry, his 19-year-old assistant; and myself—but the cup is nowhere to be found.

As I continue the search, it occurs to me that Ray owns everything in sight and more. He owns this posh RPM International Building in West Los Angeles (the ground floor of which he rents out to the Urban League). He owns this recording studio. He owns Tangerine Records, the corporation he formed in 1962 after leaving Atlantic and ABC-Paramount. And Tangerine Music and Racer Music—he owns these publishing companies too.

Tangerine's thickly carpeted, cork-lined hallways and offices glitter with Ray's gold record awards, all of them exquisitely mounted. His recent albums, *Volcanic Action of My Soul* and the one cut live with Aretha Franklin at Fillmore West, are big successes. He's been consistently honored in all the popularity polls—*Down Beat, Playboy, Jazz & Pop*—and there are young adults around who have no memory of a time when there wasn't a Ray Charles. Carol Burnett, in a *Life* story, spoke of her four-year-old daughter Jody's affection for him. "Jody goes everywhere," the comedienne remarked, "trailing a string of invisible playmates. A few days ago her father heard her ask the plumber if he had seen her children. 'I'm married to Ray Charles,' she said. 'He's a wonderful man, but he's blind, you know, and I have to lead him everywhere.'"

I grew up loving Ray, whose music helped me through some of my most difficult years.

So it is strange to see him standing here now, perspiring and smiling, feeling around for a cup of cold coffee that isn't there. Finally Tony Perry, still humming the tune that's been rocking the studio for hours now, walks out of the control booth. "I won't be back till I find it, Ray," he calls back.

When I arrived at Tangerine that morning, the first thing that struck me was a gigantic solarized photographic portrait of Ray that shines from one of the main walls of the reception room. "He's the boss of this whole operation," I found myself thinking. All the activity taking place in these offices and studios owed its existence to him, and hundreds, maybe even thousands of people were dependent upon his life and talents. It was easy to see how an industrialist might pull it off, or a

big politician. But a musician, an artist, a blind entertainer—
it seemed like a dream.

Later, while sitting in the office of Ron Granger, director
of Tangerine Records at the time, I heard a round of sunny
good mornings and songlike hellos ringing up and down the
hallway. Ray had arrived, looking rested and glowing like a
man glad to be back among old friends.

His young valet Bob Taylor had told me: "Some nights I
get Ray home by, say, two or three in the morning. I don't
have to report back to work until the following afternoon.
Well, Ray's got so much energy that he's got an a.m. man just
to help get him around town while I'm still catching up on
my sleep. He'll get his rest, wake up and read—he reads a lot
in braille—have breakfast, put in some time with Della and
the kids and then come out to the studio.

"He's got three kids, all boys. Ray, Jr., David, and Robert.
The man is beautiful. With all the stuff he's into, he still
finds time, don't ask me how, to keep up with his sons, go to a
ball game every now and then, and then turn around and put
in time on something like the Sickle Cell Anemia campaign.
He's the honorary chairman of that, you know.

"Hell, I come on the scene around three the next day and
Ray's put in a good four or five hours of work and my eyes are
still bloodshot from not getting enough sleep."

Moving unassisted through the corridors, Ray chimes out an
occasional "beep-beep" to let passers-by know he's on the
scene.

Once he reaches the recording studio, Ray takes his coat
off, calls for coffee, and paces about for several moments.
Then he pauses beside Dave Braithwaite. "Listen, make sure
everything's set up for dubbing for when Madeleine gets in
this afternoon."

"Do I have time to grab a little bite?" asks Braithwaite, a
portly, jovial man in his forties who has had more than
twenty years of broadcast and recording experience.

"What time you eat breakfast?"

"Oh, a few hours ago."

"And you mean to say you have to eat again already? You don't need to eat. That's just nervousness, man. You know what I mean?"

Ray, as I later found out, eats very little himself. He drinks several glasses of milk a day but doesn't really eat until very late at night, and then almost never in public. Ray's road manager, a soft-spoken, personable man named Don Briggs, explained his shyness about eating in public. "Restaurants are generally out," he told me. "The people, when they recognize who it is, just won't leave him alone. They want to shake his hand and get autographs. Besides, Ray's food has to be chopped up for him and he's developed special ways of eating it."

"I feel pretty good today," says Braithwaite. "Do you know that in *cinco meses* I'll be *cuarenta y cinco años* old?"

"You'll be what?" Ray asks.

"*Cuarento y cinco años* old," Braithwaite repeats playfully.

"Oh, I see." Ray nods politely and walks out to take care of some business in one of the front offices. Minutes later he strolls back in with a smiling young beauty on one arm. "I want you all to meet—ah, what'd you say your name was, dear?"

"Lucia."

"Lucia, these are my engineers, Dave and Tony. Now, Dave, what was that you were saying to me a little while ago when you were round here trying to give me the impression that you could talk Spanish? I brought somebody back that knows *all* about Spanish. She's gonna translate for me."

We all cracked up. Ray has a sly, pleasant way of never letting anything get past him. Even when he appears to be irretrievably bound up in thought, which is often, I get the impression that he's somehow aware of everything going on around him.

When Braithwaite casually mentions something about turning up the earphone amp, Ray hollers out: "Where's that located? That's something you haven't told me about. Man, you better *show* me where everything is around here!" Ray gets up and follows Braithwaite straight to the amp and gives it a thorough tactile inspection.

"Yeah," Tony Perry tells me over in one corner. "Ray likes to teach and I like to learn. He's really in a bag by himself. He doesn't follow other people. That's what I like about him. Ray's gonna do it *his* way."

Tony cues up a touching tape track called "There'll Be No Peace Without All Men As One." The singer is hauntingly original. I'm impressed and tell Tony so.

"Yeah, I love it too," he says. "Took us a long time to get all that down—the rhythm section tracks, the band, the background stuff. It's written by a lady right here in the neighborhood named Sayde Shepherd. She comes in with a few things every now and then. Ray wants to sign her as a songwriter but she always laughs and says, 'I'm just a housewife.'"

"Who's the singer?"

"Madeleine Quebec. She'll be in after lunch."

When Tony gets back with the misplaced coffee cup, it's been freshly refilled. Ray takes a steamy sip, makes a face, and lights up a Kool.

"Where'd you find Ray's cup?" Braithwaite asks Tony.

"It was in there on the piano."

Madeleine Quebec has been waiting and is ready to go. She and Ray rehearse the new song several times. Singing along with her in a remarkable falsetto, using piano chords and lines to punctuate tricky melodic and rhythmic passages, Ray emphasizes to Miss Quebec what he's after.

"See, sweetie, once more, you kinda wanna let a beat go by there before you go into this part. Now, here you try it. Yeah... Yes... Yessuh! That's what I want, baby! Let's run it through one more time and then we'll do a take. You wanna go up on this phrase here and come down on that one—keep 'em from being exactly the same. That way you don't lose the feeling. Now, this part where you sing, 'I can see you / in hurricane's eye,' I think that's wrong, hon."

"I just got these lyrics from Publishing a few minutes ago."

"Well, just sing, 'I see you / in hurricane's eye.' It's more comfortable that way. To hell with Publishing!"

It takes well over an hour for them to get the exceptionally good take that excites Ray so. He turns toward the earphoned young woman in suede hotpants, who's listening to herself being played back. "Take a break, Madeleine," he calls out gently. "That last take was good but I'd like to do a few punch-ins. Remember, after the drummer goes dom-da-dom-dom-DOM, *then* you come in. Just take your time. You have to get enough breath, honey, so you can hold that note—just grab it, dear. Don't let the drums destroy you."

Madeleine seems weary but her voice is still fresh and so is her smile, and her eyes still glisten. She's a comely, delicate-boned, Hershey-colored woman with long shiny black hair and a big expressive voice.

"OK, quiet everybody," Ray says. "We're gonna do another take and do those punch-ins. Save the other takes, Dave. There are things about each of them I like. Tony, take me to your leader!"

Tony runs the tape back to the beginning.

By late afternoon Ray is doing the engineering himself, fingering buttons, twisting knobs, calling takes, and loving every minute of it. He's as meticulous and finicky about sound textures and levels as he is about the material itself and Madeleine's performance. But once Ray finds himself delighted by what he hears, he springs to his feet, motioning for Braithwaite to take over the board. Ray rushes to the control room's glass partition and waves at Madeleine, rocking with the beat, snapping his fingers in rhythm. "Mmmmm, I love that!" he

moans, embracing himself vigorously with both arms, a ges-
ture I had thought he used only in public performance. "Joy is
over me / like radiation," he enunciates with a laugh. He claps
his sides and declares: "That's beautiful!"

Ray shouts at Madeleine (who can't hear him through
the partition): "You got it, sweetie, you got it!... Uh-uhh...
She's gonna miss this next cue, Dave, she's gonna miss it...
Whoah! I *knew* she was gonna miss it, I knew it. That's all
right, let it roll on, let her finish, we can patch that up later."

Ray's patience is extraordinary. When the take is done,
he flips on the intercom. "Madeleine, we're gonna start at the
interlude again and punch you in where we want you to go.
I'm scared to fool with that because the part's kinda tricky,
but let's try it anyway. Now, on that line, 'You arrived / just in
time,' do you understand what I was talking about before?
Can you hear it?"

"Oh yes," she answers, sounding a little like Eartha Kitt,
"I hear it... all those vowels."

"Well, you don't have to be an English major with it because I don't want it to be too pure. Where you say, 'much too
strong duration,' emphasize *much.* Say whatever you wanna
say on the fade-out but *feel* it—be true to the notes."

"Can it be a hum?"

"Whatever you want, hon, but dramatize it if you're
gonna use that word *much.*"

For the first time all day I hear Ray address Braithwaite
by his proper first name. "David, it's of the utmost importance
that you don't let me stay here past seven 'cause that's my
cue. I gotta catch a plane tonight."

The plane belongs to Ray, and the pilot and mechanics
have telephoned to say it's been checked out and is ready for
the New York flight. On the road nine months of the year,
Ray has no trouble making use of the two planes he owns—a
Viscount and a small Cessna—and he's even thinking of buy-
ing a DC-6 for transcontinental and overseas jaunts.

Ray's driver, Sam Jackson, sticks his head in the door.

"Mr. Charles, can I talk to you now?"

"No!"

"Mr. Charles," I ask, "What's the name of the song we just heard?"

"Damned if I know."

"Who wrote it?"

He turns in my direction, slightly irritated. "Damned if I know that either. Anything else I can do for you?"

Tomorrow night the band plays the Apollo in Harlem. The plane will be taking off very soon now and there's still a lot of work to be finished. I can see that he clearly doesn't wish to be interrupted again.

"All right," Ray shouts, "break's over! Madeleine, let's get ready to do it again, baby."

"How long do you think you'll be here?" I ask Tony.

"Till the very last minute. Ray doesn't believe in wasting time."

When I first heard him on record, Ray himself was imitating other singers' styles, singing in that ambiguous, bluesy Charles Brown / Nat King Cole mode that was popular in the late 1940s and early 50s. Still, from the moment I first laid ears on him—and long before the Coca-Cola people got to him—I could hear enough in that pristine style of his to know that he was, indeed, the real thing.

"Baby, Let Me Hold Your Hand" was the name of the tune that knocked me out. He cut it for a tiny west coast label called Swing Time. It hit the rhythm and blues charts in 1951 and quickly became number one. I was eleven years old and spending the summer in Pachuta, Mississippi, not very far from my hometown of Ocean Springs on the Gulf.

My cousin Jesse and I could hardly wait out the time until twilight when our grandmother, weary from farm chores, would finally retire, leaving us unsupervised in our room across the hall. Once "Mama" was asleep, bedtime was up to us. What we took pleasure in was listening to the

Randy Record Mart program as it crackled and faded in and out of our oversized Philco portable.

The Randy Record Mart Show was very special, as any lover of blues, rhythm and blues, gospel, or country and western music who remembers it will tell you. It came out of Nashville over WLAC. The disk jockey who worked the slot had one of those deep-throated voices that spun out a vein of patter that can only be described as Afro-Caucasian. The program was sponsored by the Randy Record Mart, also situated in Nashville, which specialized in mail-order merchandising. They'd offer packages: the Blues Package, the Special Gospel Package, the R&B Package, and so forth. "Just enclose cash, check or money order—no stamps, please—and tell us whether you want Randy's big Number One Special, Number Two Special, or the big Number Three, and it'll be mailed to you postage-free direct to your door or R.F.D. box anywhere within the continental United States or Canada!"

WLAC, according to pop lore, was picked up just about everywhere. I've met ex-GI's who claim to have pulled it from as far away as Seoul, Korea. For me and Cousin Jesse, it was enough that we could hear Ray Charles on it, doing "Baby, Let Me Hold Your Hand."

Ray Charles was about seventeen when he first began recording. His mother had died and he was on his own, the classic black orphan with no one to turn to. His father, a spike driver for the railroad and an all-around handyman, had been highly respected by both the black and white populations of Greenville, Florida. He died when Ray was fifteen. At the age of five, Ray had witnessed the drowning of his younger brother in a large, water-filled washtub. Ray, a year and a half older, tried to pull him out but the brother was too heavy. Their mother, who took in laundry, dropped her ironing, ran out into the backyard and tried giving him artificial respiration but it was too late.

It was Ray's mother who helped him most when, at the age of seven, glaucoma resulted in the loss of his eyesight. She didn't help him by pitying him and sheltering him from the world, but by forcing him to face up to his blindness.

Working in a lumberyard, washing and cooking for whites, she saw Ray through a St. Augustine school for the blind, where he learned music notation and arranging through braille. He also developed a mastery of piano, alto saxophone, and trumpet. He didn't have to study voice. He is blessed with perfect pitch, and singing is something he has always done. Curiously, though, he doesn't think of himself as a real singer.

"Why not?" I ask him.

"Well," he says, "I don't feel I have many of the things that voice teachers tell you you're supposed to have. Everything I do is kind of like the opposite of the way it's supposed to go. The reason I say I'm a stylist and not a singer is because I can take a note, even a note that's halfway out of tune, and bend it in such a way that it will *sound* right. But if you were to get some experts and ask, 'Is this guy a singer?' they would probably say, 'No, he's certainly not. We don't know what in the *hell* he is.'"

For a time Ray did all right for himself working the Brown-Cole vein, gigging around Florida, Tennessee and other southern states with blues bands, rhythm and blues combos, and even with a country and western band.

"There was one band," he told me, "called The Florida Playboys. I worked with them and I'll tell you something. If you could ever get a job in a band like that you would do pretty well because those guys in those days worked *all* the time. They played these little clubs and taverns and what-have-you and they always had a job. The piano player with The Florida Playboys got sick and I took his place, supposedly for one or two nights, but it wound up I stayed with them for about six months. I learned an awful lot. And I liked the music. You see, country and western music is very closely related to what we call soul, in the sense that the two musics are both very earthy. In other words, so-called country

songs—really, from the hills, you know—these are songs that
don't dress up the lyrics. They say, 'Well, I miss you, baby, so I
really went out and got drunk!' I mean, that's really what *happened.* Those songs were about everyday people. They weren't
about somebody who could pay ten dollars for a dinner."

And now—backstage after a smash performance at the Circle
Star Theater in suburban San Carlos, California— Ray
Charles is completely stripped except for his boxer shorts. He
is on his feet. "Have a seat, Al," he says. "As you can see, I'm
still pretty worked up. I have to cool down for a second."

Sweating like a long-distance runner after a meet, he
looks in excellent shape, not an ounce of flab anywhere. He
claims to have weighed the same since his middle teens—165
pounds. Without the dark glasses—he rarely wears them
when he isn't in public—he seems younger, more boyish
somehow, even though he's beginning to gray at the temples.

He responds to my questions enthusiastically, but never
without first giving them some thought. He smiles and
laughs a lot as he speaks.

"I see a lot of experimenting going on, from a technical
point of view—with machines, all kinds of equalizers, different kinds of limiters, compressors, reverb units and wah-wahs
and tremolos, and cats using oscillators to take their tracks
and put them out of phase. In other words, people are feeling,
searching to see what will catch on.

"Nowadays, for instance, the wah-wah seems to have
caught on, kind of. People seem to like that sound. But I don't
see any real *basic* change. Engineers have found out how to
get the good drum sound with the foot and the backbeat and,
of course, they're using the Fender bass now. It's always been
the rhythm section that's been the background anyway. Basie
proved that. He's been doing it for many, many years. But I
don't really see anything that's really gonna carry.

"Music, I think, for the most part, is about the same as it
was, say, thirty forty years ago. They've found better ways to

record it and they've come up with electrical instruments to *enhance* what a guy can hear and, naturally, he can do a little more with what he's felt in his head. But basically, man, that old soul from the heart, and the *reality*... for as long as I can remember I've been hearing it."

There are times when he almost sings as he talks about music. I mention veteran bluesman John Lee Hooker's remark about having played the same music for forty years while watching the name of it change.

"And, of course, that's true," Ray says, sitting down, not as noticeably wound up as before. "Because when you look at the facts, when you look at some of the youngsters—and especially the white set, the white kids—they hear this stuff and they don't know that John Lee Hooker's been around a long time. Some of them think it's something new. What happened when they were growing up is that they were not *exposed* to these people. Now that they've gotten to be of age, they go out and they buy their own records. They know that there's some other music out there that they can listen to. When they pick up a record of the Beatles or the Rolling Stones, they read their biography and they find out that these people say, 'Well, yeah, sure, this is our music but, you know, we *got* this from Muddy Waters, or from a Big Joe Turner, or from a Ray Charles.' So the young kids are curious about that and they say, 'This music is coming from over here, so maybe I'd better do a little more listening to it.'"

All this time, Ray's valet has been handing him clothing to put on.

"You see," Ray says, at last completely dressed, "you can say so many things through music. You can make people cry, you can make them think through music, and it's not distasteful. You can say things *to* a person, even *about* a person, and he will accept it because it's through music. You can say, 'Look, this is our music, and these are some of the problems we've always had. You had both my hands tied up, so you loosened one of my fingers and told me that was progress.'

You dig what I mean? Now, you can say that through music so great, man, because you can make people relate to it. I never work to the place—the Copa, the Coconut Grove, Harry's Place. I always work to the people. When you get those people in there and you get them stirred up just a little bit—it doesn't matter what kind of fur coat they've got on or what kind of diamond ring they wear—they get up and dance on the tables too."

"I saw that happening here the last couple of nights," I said.

"It's the people *always*. People are still people. We all were born and sooner or later—well, you know the end result. When you get sleepy, you wanna go to sleep. When you get thirsty, you wanna drink. And," he throws in, getting up as Don Briggs walks in with a saran-wrapped supper on a plate, "when you're hungry...."

Later Don Briggs told me about the time Ray Charles found himself on a flight to Venezuela with Colonel Sanders.

"The Colonel asked me if it would be possible to meet the Genius himself," said Briggs. "Well, I took him up front to first class and introduced him to Ray. Man, you oughtta seen the Colonel! He was in his glory, up there in his little white suit and goatee and string tie, shaking Ray's hand and all up in his face about how he'd been a fan of Ray's for years and years. He was like some little kid!"

I never got around to telling Don Briggs about the time I went to visit a friend on the ward of a California hospital. Like the other patients and callers, my buddy Wardess Taylor and I were whiling away visiting hours, yakking away the countdown to bedcall, when suddenly the whole lounge quieted down as all heads snapped toward a TV set in one corner. A matronly nurse, responding to whispers of *shhh*, stepped over and turned up the volume.

The magnetic face that glowed on the screen belonged to Ray Charles, one of the most dynamically influential performing musicians America has ever produced, and surely one of the few people anywhere capable of mesmerizing that particular hospital area.

   We all stared silently, almost reverently, at the legendary black man seated at the piano on TV. Ray Charles was delivering a ballad so soulfully and moving that it caused Wardess to turn, touching my arm, and say, "Man, this is better than all the doctoring and shrinking these people've been laying on me since I signed myself into this joint."

the barber
of seville

GIOACHINO ANTONIO ROSSINI, COMPOSER

Possibly because of the Lone Ranger who, as any seasoned Detroiter will tell you, originated from the local studios of radio station WXYZ, I got on a Rossini kick one summer and devoured his work, even though I wasn't naturally drawn to opera. But I was playing tuba and sometimes baritone horn, instruments my father had played professionally in his youth, in the Central High School Band. I was also studying trumpet on the side. In addition to the usual marches, light classics and cutesy-poo pop, the band was playing modified arrangements of Schubert's *Unfinished*, Tchaikovsky's *Nutcracker Suite*, and Ravel's *Bolero*.

Every time Mr. Kurtez, the band conductor, stepped out of the room, we would rag and jazz whatever score we happened to be rehearsing with the kind of sneering irreverence that adolescents the world over savor. It was the same spirit that, sheltered in large auditorium groups, prompted us to sing, "Walking in My Winter Underwear" instead of "Walking in a Winter Wonderland." Or, on the sly, to open "The Star Spangled Banner" with the words: "O say can you see / Any bedbugs on me? / If you do / Pick a few / And I'll fry them for you." The chorus of singer Lloyd Price's winning rhythm & blues tune, "Personality," had to do with someone having personality and great big heart to boot. Inevitably, gathered in freewheeling locker-room chorales, we sang: "'Cause you got / Personality / Personality / Plus you got a great big ha-aarr-rrd!" When Jack "Dragnet" Webb's former wife Julie London came out with "Cry Me a River," we faithfully transformed it into "Fry Me a Liver." There was even one tiresomely clever, if not brilliant, lad who had nothing better to do than change the entire score of the Broadway musical *Guys and Dolls* into an off-color, pubescent parody by substituting his own dumb, smutty lyrics for Frank Loesser's. It seems that no matter how busy they're kept, teenagers somehow find plenty of time to cut up and be silly.

In the middle of my teens, during my summertime Rossini Period, and probably crazed by my determination to get at the essence of *The Barber of Seville*, which I was listening to repeatedly, I decided to give myself a haircut. Undetected by the rest of the family, I stood in front of the bathroom mirror, shaving my head with an electric razor that once belonged to an uncle who used to cut the family hair. There I shaved and shaved away, trying to create a proper design. Gradually I succeeded in shearing myself bald: so bald, in fact, that I could see the ridges and humps in my own scalp.

They resembled little plow rows of the skull. I screamed in terror and, delighted at the same time, rushed out to either buy or find a hat. In all likelihood, I dug up the hat in our attic where all the throw-away clothes that hadn't or couldn't be passed on were stored.

Painfully vain, I wore that old slouch hat for most of the summer, only taking it off to sleep. Girls and even my friends laughed at me. Shaved heads were in fashion in a modest way, even in the distant, dark Fifties, but mine looked ridiculous. My mother thought it so funny that she snickered at me continuously and defiantly. I didn't have to get another haircut for months, and when I finally did it wasn't because I wanted to but, rather, because my stepfather mashed the money into my hand and said, "For Chrissake, please go get some of that mess cut offa your head!"

I might've been dumb, but I never pulled that number again. About the closest I've ever come since has been the time or two that I've compulsively shaved off my mustache without truly meaning to, and on each occasion it was almost as though some mischievous, tramp spirit had stepped into my body to take possession.

Rossini himself, more than likely, knew a little something about the value of impulsive acts. Early in his lucrative career he settled for a spell in Bologna where he struck up a deal with the theater and gambling casino impresario, Barbaja. As it turned out, Rossini had to knock out one opera a year for the Teatro San Carlo and the Teatro del Fondo at Naples. For good measure, he was also cut in on a piece of the action at Barbaja's gaming tables. Besides producing a string of hits, Signor Rossini hit it off beautifully with his courtly and aristocratic groupies both in Italy and abroad. His first wife was a successful singer; his last, a cultured French studio model. Retiring to France, he still had plenty of time to disengage himself and look back on it all with witty indifference, detachment and humility.

Looking back on my ephemeral involvement with *The*

Barber of Seville, I can't help but dwell on my old hair and that floppy old hat. Both are like dreams to me now. I also can't help wondering whatever happened to the hat once it got out of my hands. Did it curiously find its way to Detroit's old Skid Row, then on perhaps to Boston's Scollay Square, the Bowery in Manhattan, Denver's Larimer Street, or the Mission in San Francisco? How did its smell change? Maybe some little boy once donned it comically with a flower plucked out of someone's yard to amuse a little girl.

What's become of that garment and all the old shirts, shoes, trousers, and sweaters, all the apparel of the passing flow? Where does it all end up—old dreams, old music, old songs, fleeting enthusiasms and, of course, all that shorn hair that was once alive? Where, pray tell, have I gone since? For fun, I could wear that slouch hat tonight for a few minutes and think about all my ungainly transformations. I'd stand in front of the bathroom mirror and laugh at myself, at how utterly foolish I was then and still am, and I'd laugh at how I, just like that crumply headpiece, remain completely silly, beside the point, and unconcernedly beautiful.

Just think about it.

Today, there are still more people around who remember the Lone Ranger, his horse Silver, his faithful Indian companion Tonto, and his arch-enemy Butch Cavendish when they hear the *William Tell Overture* than there are faithful listeners to Rossini's grand and rigidly formal opera.

You never know. Satchel Paige was right again: "Don't look back; something might be gaining on you."

in a mist

BIX BEIDERBECKE, 1927

Play it one more time, Bix, so I can cascade down your water-
fall of tears and up again all on my own.

I can tell by the silence of the notes you aren't hitting
that your head's getting funny again from sitting up all night,
every night, night after night, banking on bad speak booze to
navigate you through seas of sound on boats that leave but
never dock, at least never long enough to unload your steamy
cargo—a love affair with sound itself, and what it can and
cannot do.

Tell me, Bix, jazz darling, legendary refugee from Iowa and Cincinnati Oom-Pah-Pah, is there really any difference (besides time, that is) between your 1920s twenties and the twenties of Nineteen Now? All that appetizing ear food, those saucy, futuristic chords you cook up on piano to go, and heat back up on cornet—where, if anywhere, will it end up? Better than any physicist, you already know that time, space, motion, stillness, distance and nearness are one. What you're deep into now is the whirling of planets as notated by Gustav Holst, your favorite composer after Louis Armstrong: the sibilant motion of heavenly bodies, and the whispering of the hours going by and by and by.

Tell me, doesn't that same lonesome-looking moon still pull, bringing women around in a cycle as different from man-made lunacy as bathwater from gin? And isn't what you've always loved and dreamed still as American as aspirin, or atomic secrets; as American as apple pie frozen in color on a television screen?

That's the part of music's mystery they're going to have to get a law out against: your secret ingredient, your mystical spray capable of shattering whole cities and countrysides while—unlike a neutron bomb—it leaves listeners intact, craving infinity. Your spirit need only be there, contained inside the mystery.

I, they, you, we—we all need your mistiness, Bix. Play it again please, won't you? Again and again and again—life is so long, and always too short.

black brown and beige

DUKE ELLINGTON ORCHESTRA, 1947

(or, miz chapman tells us the score)

"Now son, I know you can do better than that. You've *got* to do better. You know how come? Because you're black, that's why. Nothing's going to come easy in this world that's laying for you out there, so you might as well get used to having to be twice as good as white folks at whatever you do if you intend to ever make anything out of yourself."

The woman speaking wasn't my mother. It was Miz Chapman, my second-grade teacher at Kingston Primary

School for Colored in Laurel, Mississippi, 1947. My mother, who later bombarded me with similar warnings, was still quite young then. Unable to look after and provide for all of her children, she had sent me and a much younger brother back from Detroit to our native state to spend a couple of years with her sister, my Aunt Doris, and her family. This practice wasn't unusual then, long before such notions as the Nuclear Family, the Civil Rights Struggle and Black Pride were widespread.

Zora Neale Hurston, the late and eminent novelist and folklorist, spoke of being "passed around the family like a bad penny." Perhaps because I was only seven at the time, I didn't feel as though I were being farmed out. Still, it felt peculiar to be separated from my true parents—that is until I landed in Miz Chapman's room in that big, dilapidated, gray wooden structure surrounded by mud.

She was indeed a remarkable woman, this scolder and molder of minds, this Miz Chapman. Dark-skinned, white-haired, scalding of eye and seemingly telepathic, she was often given to warm laughter. Moreover, she possessed an uncanny ability, common to the elderly in those days, of being able to train her laser-like sight on your very soul. With a look that variously melted or chilled, Miz Chapman was capable of reading everything there was to know about you—past, present or future—at a glance. And she was memorably tough on her secret favorites, pupils from whom she expected nothing short of excellence. Unfortunately, I happened to be one of those.

One chilly Friday morning in late autumn, while we were putting away our readers and bringing out arithmetic homework, Miz Chapman casually announced that anyone who wanted to stick around after school to "learn a little something about the history of the Negro race" was welcome to do so. "It's important that you all know about that," she added.

Given all the activities, sanctioned and unsanctioned,

that went on after school in our sad little corner of that textile mill and cannery town, I was surprised to find myself remaining after classes had let out just to learn what Miz Chapman had to teach us. Leontyne Price, a native of Laurel, might have been weaving her girlish, operatic dreams at that very moment. Since it was all entirely voluntary—and that went for our teacher's time as well—only a handful of us had been curious enough to take up the invitation.

Drawing a long face, the twinkle never leaving her eye, Miz Chapman gave us each a special look, then seated us in a semicircle around the rotund wood heater, now grown cold, that squatted in one corner of the rickety room. Chilly, we had to keep on our coats and jackets and sweaters. This arrangement, of course, was far more intimate than when she presided over us from her mean-looking desk up front by the blackboard.

"You poor things," she began, removing her glasses and pinching the bridge of her nose. "Poor babies. I wish there were more of you here because this here is something you really need to know about. We'll just have to start where we have to. Nothing makes a failure but a trial."

Those cryptic, prefatory remarks of Miz Chapman's were making me giddy with anticipation. I was innocently fascinated and yet, at the same time, slightly frightened. What on earth was she about to tell us that was so important that she found it necessary to lower her voice so mysteriously, so ominously?

"I reckon we'll have to begin with slavery," she said. "Now, you all know about slavery, don't you?"

Some of us knew vaguely about slavery and some of us didn't. It must be remembered that public school classrooms back then were often filled with pupils of varying ages. Not everyone was automatically passed on the way they are now, and certainly not in Miz Chapman's class. You simply had to master the material she was teaching before she would advance you to the next grade. There was no getting around it.

In that second-grade class of hers, there were kids old enough to be third-graders, and several lanky, strapping ones of fourth, fifth or possible sixth grade age.

"Miz Chapman, ma'am," I raised my hand and asked, "would you please explain what slavery was?"

She folded her hands in her lap and leaned forward on her chair. "There was a time—and it wasn't all that long ago either—when colored people were in slavery. That was how we started out, in this country anyway, in these United States, this place we call America."

A stickler for correct speech and grammar, Miz Chapman, in her role as teacher, customarily spoke in gentle, cultivated Southern tones. Her voice was musical and proper when she wanted it to be. Naturally, she was also very much one of the people: a public servant who was on familiar terms with practically everybody in the community. She knew who your parents or guardians were and made a point of socializing with them as regularly as she could. In fact, chances were better than reasonable that she'd taught them when they were children. At the drop of a ruler, she could shift linguistic gears and become vigorously—if not wickedly—colloquial when the occasion called for it.

There was many a youngster, myself included, who knew what it was like to look up and blink just in time to duck an oncoming blackboard eraser hurled at top speed by Miz Chapman herself right at your unsuspecting head. "Next time I'll take better aim," she might shout down the aisle of desks at the offender. "Since you so doggone hardheaded, maybe that's the only way I can get through to you. Don't worry. I *will* get through!" Those old erasers weren't the soft felt kind in use today. They were chalky strips of heavy cloth glued to hard blocks of wood. Used accurately as missiles, they could cause severe concussions.

This afternoon, however, nobody was fooling around. We were all giving Miz Chapman our best attention. The message that she was warming up to was as clear and cold as ice water.

"Slavery," she continued, rising from her seat and pointing, "is when you—and by you I do mean *you, you* and *you*—are owned by somebody else, the same way somebody might own a dog or a cat or a mule or a cow. Now, the way the Creator meant for things to go, there wasn't supposed to be any such thing as slavery. People all over the world, all they are is brothers and sisters. But we don't always go by God's laws. We're like a world full of wayward children. We forget about the Lord and do things our way, and what that means is any old kinda way."

She paced around the heater momentarily, as though pulling her urgent thoughts together, "People out of Spain, England, France, Holland and different places, they hopped in their little boats and sailed over here to start them up a new country, so they say. Now, you all remember when we were studying about Christopher Columbus and the Pilgrims and all those folks? Remember how the Indians were already here when they stepped off the boat? Well, keep that in mind because that's important. We'll get back to that and talk about it some more because all that fits in with what I'm fixing to tell you."

Somewhere down inside my stomach, a little knot was beginning to tighten. I looked around at the other faces to see how my classmates were taking this old woman's words. Like the rest of this motley assemblage, I had seen my share of western movies, but had never stopped to consider why the Indians were always going on the warpath, or why Tom Mix, Bob Steele, Hopalong Cassidy and other cowboy heroes were forever shooting at them. Everybody sat engrossed, entranced and wide-eyed.

"You see," said Miz Chapman, peeping around furtively before sitting again, "you can go buy yourself a mule and hitch that mule up to pull your wagon or plow your land. You don't have to pay that mule a salary. All you have to do is give him feed and give him water, and maybe have a barn or a shed to put him in at night or when the weather gets rough. I mean, who ever heard of a mule or a cow or a chicken drawing a paycheck?"

When she broke out into a smile, we all knew that it was OK to follow her lead. We smiled back and a couple of us laughed nervously.

"Wellsir," she went on, "Back in those days, going way, way back—three four hundred years at least—you could buy yourself a person. That's right, a person, a human being, a man, a woman, a child—depending on what you needed 'em for—and you could train that person and put 'em to work just like you might any other poor beast of burden. And that's what was done with us. Slavetraders—men who made their living catching and selling slaves—traveled all up and down the coast of Africa, packing their slaveships with the strongest men and women and little bitty children they could round up and bringing 'em back over here to sell."

"But why'd they have to go all the way over there?" some girl wanted to know. "Couldn't they capture 'em some white folks and Indians right here?"

Miz Chapman shook her head and smiled again. "Whoa, now, that's a good question! Bless your heart! Shows me you got your thinking cap on. What you say! Fact of the matter is they did have a right sizeable few of their own kind in slavery all along. There used to be something called debtors prison. You owe so much money and can't pay off your debts and bills. Well, over yonder in England, say, they might slap you in prison and then you might could work out a deal where you'd get shipped over here to the Colonies and be put in slavery—indentured servitude, they called it—until you worked off what you owed. But, you see, white folks, it looked like, could always buy their way out of slavery somehow, but the Negro couldn't, not in most places anyway. You have to remember something, though—and if you don't remember this, then nothing else I'm trying to tell you today'll make much sense—so pay attention. White folks won't treat us the same way they treat other white folks. Listen at what I'm saying.

White folks treat colored people different. They always have, and they still do!"

"And the Indians?" I asked.

"This Indian," she said, shaking her head. "Seems like they never could get him to work for them the way they could us. See, child, it's one thing when you pile in and take over somebody else's country, and another thing when you go yanking people from out their home and drag and carry 'em off someplace that's thousands of miles across the ocean, put 'em in chains, then dare 'em to run away or do anything about their condition. That's how they did us. They snatched us up the way you might go out in the woods and catch a rabbit or a possum or a squirrel, then they pent and cooped us up. They put us to planting cotton, chopping cotton, picking cotton, cooking, sewing, scrubbing, building, mending, riding shotgun on one another and every other kinda chore you can think of, even raising their little privileged children and—"

"But why?" It was the same girl's voice interrupting her. "I need to know why!"

"Girl, I already told you! It was cheaper to do it that way than it was to pay somebody, that's why. It's always cheaper to make somebody work for you for nothing than it is to pay 'em."

Miz Chapman's gaze turned suddenly toward the row of tall windows in back of us—kept sparkling clean by pupils forced to work off violations—where the late afternoon light had begun to fade.

"You know," she told us, getting to her feet, "for all that, we're still here. We are still here. We're still struggling, but we're still here. Y'all know that old spiritual we sing about 'I Been 'Buked and I Been Scorned'? Well, for all that, for all they have done to us and're trying to do to us, we are still here, right here, carrying on... still trying to make that journey home."

Her face softened wistfully. A tear slipped down one of her tall cheekbones. "Everything they could see to take away from us, they took. They took away our homeland, our families and the people we loved, our language, our customs, our music, our history.... But you know what? All we are is children of God, and the Almighty will take care of His own. No need for you to worry about *that*. Just like He parted the waters of the Red Sea and led the Israelites out of bondage in Egypt, the Lord is looking after all of His children.

"And for everything they took away, we came up with something new. We commenced to making a new religion. We sang us some new songs and danced us some new dances. We created new families, built us some new homes, and commenced to making some new history, too. See, you can put a hurting on the body, but you can't touch the soul. You know how come that is? It's because the soul of man, the same as God's love, is everlasting. The Good Book says, 'And I will dwell in the house of the Lord *forever*'!

"Now, it also says in the Good Book that God helps those who help themselves, and that's just what we've been doing and what we're bound to do more of. The way we go about doing that is first by learning *how* we can help ourselves. You young 'uns have opportunities we didn't have when I was coming along. You can go to school and study. You all are in a position to do a whole lot more than we could. But you're still dealing with the same situation. You don't have to be all that smart to look around at the way we're being treated and cheated to see that we aren't a free people yet. No, not yet.

"I feel like it's part of my job to tell you all what I know about what our people have been through before you got here, before you were born. I want you all to know about the Negro race and some of the people, *great* people, who didn't sit around and lay around waiting for somebody else to get busy. There were some who saw what had to be done, who went on ahead and did it, and what they did *stayed* done! I'm talking about folks like Phillis Wheatley, Harriet Tubman, Sojourner Truth, Frederick Douglass, Paul Laurence Dunbar,

Booker T. Washington, W.E.B. DuBois, George Washington Carver, Mary McCleod Bethune, A. Philip Randolph, Langston Hughes, and plenty other Negro geniuses you aren't liable to find out too much about in history books these white folks put out."

One older boy seated next to me screwed up his face and raised his hand. "Miz Chapman," he asked, "how come white folks so doggone mean?"

"Now, that's something you've got to be careful about," she told him. "Not everybody's the same. Even with white folks, some're different. You can't go putting good white folks, quality white folks, in the same category as crackers and peckerwoods. Y'all are old enough to know by now that there's a big difference between good and bad anything. If it wasn't for good-thinking white folks, then the Underground Railroad wouldn't have worked as well as it did."

"The Underground Railroad," I asked. "What was that?"

"I see we have a lot of catching up to do," said Miz Chapman. "That's why I want you all to listen and think about some of this stuff I'm telling you, then I want you to come back here with some questions. You know, there's such a thing as slavery of the mind too. You have to think. Next time we meet, we'll be talking about some of these Negro geniuses, like, now, you take Dr. George Washington Carver. By the way, who can tell me who he was?"

A girl raised her hand. "He invented the peanut, didn't he?"

Miz Chapman laughed. "No, child, he didn't exactly *invent* the peanut, but you're on the right track. George Washington Carver took the common little peanut, studied it real hard, then did things with it that people all over the world are still benefiting by. He was a botanist, one of our great scientists known the world over. Fact of business, he just died a few years ago over in Tuskegee. And when people would ask him how he got to know so much, Dr. Carver would explain how important it was to study, *and* to have faith in the Lord. It was by listening to God that he was able to figure out so much and get to be so great.

"All of us are children of God, don't care what anybody else tells you—and before you turn grown, you'll be hearing a whole gang of explanations about how the world was created and how mankind got here. You just take your strength from the Almighty, trust in Him, use your own good sense and go on about your business. Anybody with any kind of sense knows good and well that man did *not* make this world and the stars and the planets and the seasons and all that comes with it. This earth is our home for *now*, that's all. We just pass through here on our way someplace else. But, see, that doesn't mean we won't have to fight for what we have a right to. There are going to be trials and there are going to be tribulations. Nobody's going to give you a durn thing! When they wrote the Constitution, white folks weren't thinking about us because Negroes were considered the same as property and livestock. 'Kill a mule and I'll hire another'n; kill a nigger and I'll buy another'n!' That's how the old saying went. But after the Civil War and President Abraham Lincoln signed the Emancipation Proclamation, that was a step in the right direction. Yet and still, nobody's going to just walk up and hand you nothing for free. You've got to work and struggle for it, and most times you've got to fight for it. 'Here, old So-and-So, we want you to have this here freedom on accounta you all right with us.' Hunh, what you say? That isn't how it works. You have got to earn it; but before you can earn, first you have to learn. Get something in your head and then—no matter what they do to you; no matter how lowdown the world becomes—they can't knock it out of you! But you can't operate on muscle and nerve and brains alone. You need heart; you need God. You need the Master to lean on and guide you."

Then, rising and resting her hands in the pockets of her well-worn coat, Miz Chapman looked at the wall clock and said, "Now, who wants to lead us in reciting the 'Twenty-Third Psalm'?"

Looking back now from a vantage point of some thirty-odd years, it's easy to see how there must have been countless Miz Chapmans in Black classrooms all over the country who loved their calling devotedly, and who strove to give Black, Brown and Beige children charged to their care the skills, both practical and spiritual, that they would be needing to build halfway meaningful lives for themselves in a society that has traditionally spurned and rejected their kind. From that day on, I heeded such shibboleths as "What you get in your head, nobody can knock out." I heard them echoed so repeatedly, in fact, that they began to sound platitudinous. The vividness, however, of Miz Chapman's pronouncements at the first of those after-school study sessions has lasted.

I remember that it was growing dark as I made my way home from the schoolyard. Clutching my books wrapped in grocery bag paper, I hurried along the dirt roadways and partially asphalted paths, cutting across trash-strewn vacant lots and fields of weeds, leaping over sluggish puddles and mud holes, some of them rumored to be mined with quicksand.

"Yea, though I walk through the valley of the shadow of death, I will fear no evil; for Thou art with me . . . ."

Finally I was sprinting past the broken-down fences and ramshackle houses of my own little block in that part of Laurel known as Kingston Bottom.

"Thou preparest a table before me in the presence of mine enemies . . ."

The smell of suppers cooking filled the air. I could see lights burning in the windows of our place, the last house on the road before you came to the creek. My Aunt Doris would be inside where it was warm, preparing a meal of neckbones and rice, turnip greens, cornbread, molasses, buttermilk. To top it all off, there'd be no school tomorrow!

I didn't know exactly yet who "mine enemies" were but, like the distant croaking of frogs hidden in darkness by the creek, I knew that they were out there somewhere, crouched, setting their traps, laying for me like wild game hunters. And

I knew that I was either going to learn to be strong, clever and swift, or forever play dead.

A surge of pure joy was bubbling inside me as I raced down the final stretch home.

what a dream

SIDNEY BECHET & HIS ORCHESTRA, 1938

While I was chasing a typewriter, Michael Frimkas was busy
chasing his horn. Mike was a Berkeley neighbor trained to be
a sculptor, but what he really wanted to do was shape and
play with sound. So he bought himself a saxophone, a soprano, which was just beginning to come back in vogue in the
early 1960s. Sidney Bechet had made a name for himself years
ago playing that difficult instrument. But Sidney Bechet had
repaired to Paris, become a French national hero, and no one

seemed to take the soprano saxophone seriously until John Coltrane came out with his smash recording of "My Favorite Things" in 1960.

Well, Mike went a little crazy when he heard that record. He rushed out and bought himself a sleek, shiny pawnshop soprano. He bought the thing and left it in its case in one corner of his studio, taking it out every once in a while to admire its intricate symmetry. Almost two years went by before he got to looking at it seriously one afternoon and decided that he wanted to learn to play it. The time had come. I watched him go through this change from a distance, for I was quite sociable in one sense in those crazy days, but I was also given to sullen stretches of hunger for pure privacy. The idea was to mold myself into a real writer, word by word, line by line, day by day. I was nervously seeking inspiration everywhere, in everything, and yet I knew that ultimately I was going to have to be the source of my own inspiration. As I recall, I had hand-printed a few lines of Kenneth Patchen's that went something like this: Writing begins when you would rather be doing anything else, and just have been.

Three months after Mike had begun to take up his horn in earnest, he suspended his sculpting, stopped making love to his woman and took to propping up his energy—or so he believed—with alcohol and other drugs. For days on end he did nothing but toodle on that horn. And he was absolutely dreadful. I can remember the feeling of lazy spring afternoons when I would hang out my window and listen to his sad efforts at being completely spontaneous as he struggled to run with it before he was even ready to crawl. Poor fellow, I thought, at least he knows how to mold clay and chip stone, plus he can always teach if economic push comes to shove.

Then one splendid summer afternoon, after Berkeley's fragrant plum blossoms had turned to fruit and seed again, I was in my kitchen, right across the yard from where Mike lived. I heard him singing, *singing* on his instrument. Mike had triumphed. Not only could he crawl; he could walk, and at a very brisk pace. Suddenly he was playing beautifully. I couldn't get over it. His self-confidence, to say nothing of competence, seemed remarkable. What an electrifying moment that was for me, listening to him trill and cavort around in different keys, actually playing the blues while I went about chopping onions and garlic for a big pot of beans I was making.

When I saw him on the street some days afterwards, I told Mike how impressed I'd been with his progress.

"I'm a mess," he told me. "Lost my old lady and my health's shot from going without sleep, but I know what I have to do now. The fear's gone. That's the best thing about it. The fear's disappeared."

It would be wonderful to be able to go on and tell about how Mike eventually made a name for himself in the music world. He didn't. He went back to sculpting and, although I've heard second-hand that he hasn't done badly at it, the fact I care about is that our lives intersected at a vital point where I was able to learn something from him. And what was that? Just this: it's possible to flower at anything you really want to do well simply by planting yourself in it and becoming a fanatic, totally, completely. That's what I started doing after I watched him do it, or rather, heard him.

Before I moved, Michael Frimkas made a winning ceramic ashtray and handed it to me as a gift. It's been in the family for years now and always when I wash it clean and let it dry, its blue and gray gloss comes out and I admire its swirly edges. I also think about Mike whenever I play Sidney Bechet, which isn't every day, but often enough to remind me how original true music always is.

I'm still busy chasing this typewriter and living to tell about it.

what now my love

HERB ALPERT & THE TIJUANA BRASS, 1965

Imagine me, not exactly one of our favorite sons, pulling up as
usual on the San Diego bus via San Ysidro to that little wire
fence where a brown-shirted cop on the U.S. side once told
me that he had never, in fifteen years of working that post,
been across the border to Mexico—which to him was one big
Tijuana—and never would. That was in the very early Sixties.
He made me and Bob Mates, my travel companion at the
time, produce what Bob called "I.D. up the kazoo" to prove we

hadn't been in jail and weren't secret gangsters, part of the kiddy underworld.

Now it's three years later, 1965. Haight Ashbury is going on: lysergic acid, the ubiquitous Beatles, Timothy Leary, Richie Havens, The Lovin' Spoonful, Ravi Shankar, gurus, the Black Panthers, Ornette Coleman, the Sexual Freedom League, witchcraft, communes, riots, copulation in the streets, the Rolling Stones, Bob Dylan, macrobiotics, dashikis, enormous Afros, Otis Redding, bell-bottoms, fat belts with big buckles, apocalyptic chit-chat, secret home arsenals and Vietnam.

This time I get off the bus just when it's turning dark. There isn't anyone guarding anything at the border, so I'm free to walk across like the proverbial human being. A fat customs official checks the tourist papers that've been typed up so nicely for me at the Mexican Consulate on Market Street in San Francisco only days before. Everything's in order. The show is on. From here on out, I'm thinking, it's going to be Mexico and How It Got that Way—for a little while anyway, for a few dreams at least.

Then the oddest things begin to happen—odd enough to make me think to examine my own lopsided karma, or what I believe to be just that, being newly curious about the realness of God's laws. I behold the smoking taxi driver that a little boy leads me to in the drizzling night. This driver, he don't say nothing when I climb into his cab, not until we shoot out from customs and down the block toward the bus station; then suddenly he breaks into that local lingo, the Tijuanese, yakking all about how things've been, cha-cha-cha, and *quien sabe?* and *po siiii* and *gringuistas* and who knows what all? Having at first taken me to be a true Latino of some kind, he's made to realize by my muffled replies in Spanish that either (a) I've been out of practice speaking the language for some time now, or (b)—and more probably—that I must be that occasional *gringo negro* who slips across the border, usually from the San Diego Naval Yard to either get high or get laid, and this cabbie's determined to get all he can out of the deal.

"How much?" I ask when we're safely in front of the Three Gold Star bus station (*Tres Estrellas de Oro*).

Still rapping, as talk was hiply called then, in Baja Californian, he breaks out into an attitude that's plainly North American. He says, "*Tres dólares.*"

"Three dollars! For what? You must mean three pesos!"

Nope, he don't mean that at all. He means three dollars—*tres dólares*. "Want me to write it out, *señor*?"

Now, to be honest, I've been counting on that three dollars, which was all I had in sheer cash in my pocket, to get me through one or two days on the road at those upcoming bus-ride meal stops, but no—now it's going to be poured down that hole in the hand that everybody's holding out for the *yanqui* dollah. I stutter and sputter, but the cabbie will have none of it. "Can't you take a dollar? That's really all I've got."

"*Lo siento, señor, pero no lo pue'o!*"—(Nope, sorry, I can't!)

We retreat into quietude while I realize that huge clops of rain are bombarding the taxi top. "Can you at least wait till I go inside and cash a traveler's check?"

"They won't cash a traveler's check in there."

"Then where?"

"Nowhere, *señor*."

How come he's got to lie like that for a rudimentary three bucks? But then again, I had lied by claiming not to have that much money. We each wait it out until finally I can't stand it. I want to be out of this dreaded Tijuana and back into what to me is the real Mexico, so I hand him the three U.S. dollars, my last. This leaves me with close to fifty or sixty cents to blow as I wish.

My thoughts of the moment go something like this:

This middleaged gent with the pudgy form and gray mustachios probably has eight kids at home and they all want new leather coats, transistor radios and racing bikes for presents, constantly and on a rotating basis. Besides, there's that familiar menacing stare I've come to recognize down here as meaning: "You fatuous person, *oye!* We know you've got all the money in the world, don't care what you say. Otherwise, how come it is you're able to be vacationing down South of the Border when the only way we get up there on the up and up's when your Secretary of Labor signs a bill with ours saying it's OK to ship, to sheep like peegs, *señor*, like cattle, so many thousands of *braceros* to pick your stupid sun-kissed oranges, your grapes, your beans, onions, tomatoes, asparagus, lettuce, your harvests that go into cans and deep-freezes for shiny supermarket shelves and displays so that Joe Dog and Nancy Bitch can pull up in new cars to run inside and grab a can of Libby's or Del Monte's on special as advertised in order to heat that queek meal for deener for the family to smack its lips upon and then go *burp*, Bromo Seltzer, and fade out in front of the news flashing over the TV that's in everybody's brand new house. We know all about it. We have to look at your TV and movies too and read *Time* and *Newsweek*. So you see, *señor*, you must cough up, like you say, the *dinero*, in order that I might nourish my own thin family."

The cabbie's attitude doesn't change one drop as I hand over the loot, resolving in my head to tell everyone I run across who's headed this way in the future not to take a taxi but to *walk* the three blocks from the border to the bus station.

I strain to picture myself as this ruthless taxi driver, and what's amazing is that I actually can, whereupon from my lips cometh the words, *"Vaya con Diós, señor."* Of course, I'm aware that I've bypassed the pop sentimental meaning of this phrase of parting (popularized in Les Paul and Mary Ford's hit record of the early 1950s) and penetrated its gut spiritual origin. I say it with just the slightest hint of an undertone, perhaps an overtone that translates: "See, you treat me as if I were a murderous, fat, capitalist lackey, and yet I think enough of you to express my humble blessings for your well-being."

As for the cabbie, well, he smiles. He smiles, folding the dirty, pitiful dollars away, making them disappear sleight-of-hand style. And what does he tell me? Smiling, he twists in his seat and says, "And may God be with you too, *amigo.*"

Zapped now, I collect my bags and go blow my last few coins on milk and a tunafish roll, a *torta,* at the station snack counter. The man in the ticket cage listens to my story, then explains my predicament to the young bus driver personally. Fortunately for me, this driver's a gentle man.

"*Pues,*" he saith unto me, "you're gonna have trouble cashing any traveler's checks before we get into the south—to Mazatlán anyway, maybe even as far as Guadalajara. You see, the counterfeiting of such documents has become so commonplace that nobody'll take them any more up this way. So why don't you just get on the bus and ride anyway? By and by we'll get your checks cashed for you, yes? Also, my friend, you'll be needing a little money for eating along the way, will you not? Here you have fifty pesos I'm lending you. You pay me back when you cash your check, OK?"

This is what's known as goodness, and it is all that holds Creation together.

black pearls

JOHN COLTRANE, 1958

In the spring of 1957, half crazy with hunger for the whole sad world, I hitched a ride from Detroit to New York to wander the streets of that fabled city, probably to prove to myself that it actually existed but also to see where much of the music I loved was coming from. Music to me, then as now, represented a higher reality, a luminous touchstone, my polar connection, one of the only real reasons for staying alive.

Checking in at the Sloane House Y on West 34th Street, I

walked and subwayed everywhere, keeping a nightly diary of my doings and sightings, wolfing down my daily meal in lonely automats or at hotdog & papaya drink stands. I even had the nerve to ring up famous musicians such as Horace Silver and Thelonious Monk whose numbers I was shocked to find listed in the Manhattan directory. What a romantic time I thought I was having as rain poured down and my ten-day stash of quarters and dimes trickled down to nickels.

I actually faked my way into jazz clubs, Birdland mostly, which wasn't all that hard to do since I was seventeen but seemed older and the local drinking age was eighteen. Seated in Birdland's gallery one drizzly off-night, a Monday, I got into a beery conversation with a portly, talkative, older jazz fiend who thought he knew everything about the music by dint of being a New Yorker. He was really what they called in those days a hippie although the term didn't yet carry its later, more complicated, connotation.

We were listening, Mr. Talk and I, to a quartet led by tenor saxophonist Teo Macero who would later become Miles Davis' producer at Columbia. I was fond of a little ten-inch album Macero had cut on bassist/composer Charles Mingus' Debut label. Between sets the subject of tenor players came up as it usually did in those jazz-as-contest days.

It just so happened that a splendid young horn man named Sonny Rollins was carving a solid reputation for himself as the champion tenorist of the day, the man most likely to inherit the silver cup that had been passed around among such legendary forerunners as Coleman Hawkins, Ben Webster and Lester Young. Mr. Talk, to hear him tell it, had personally known and dug them all and could elaborate at length on the fine points of their respective careers right on down to the catalog numbers of labels they'd recorded for. I was impressed and intimidated.

"What do you think of this man Trane?" he asked finally.

"John Coltrane? I like him very much—at least from what little I've heard of him on record with Miles. He's got a strong, soulful sound. There's a lot of the blues in there. You don't forget it."

Cookin', the first of four unforgettably brilliant Miles Davis Quintet LPs—all of them taped, as I later learned, in two all-day sessions the year before—had just been released. Practically everyone I knew back around Detroit had been turned around by the band's sound and by Coltrane in particular. Paul Chambers, the quintet's bassist, was from Detroit, a highly jazz-conscious city at the time.

"Let me tell you something," Mr. Talk went on. "Keep an eye on this dude Coltrane. The man is definitely into something. I don't think he's really got himself completely together yet, but look out! I've been watching him for a couple of years now, ever since he hooked up with Miles. He keeps getting stronger and stranger by the minute."

"How do you mean?"

"How do I mean?" Mr. Talk laughed and took a very long sip from his latest drink. "Ha! You haven't caught that band in person yet?"

True, I hadn't. Back in Michigan you still had to be twenty-one to get into a club.

"Well, when you finally do catch Trane live on the set, you'll hear exactly what I mean. He plays that horn of his to death! He's all up under it and all on top of it. He takes long runs that wear me out just listening. Sometimes it's almost like he's woodshedding right up there on the stand, practicing scales and exercises and stuff. He's after something. I don't know what it is, but I sure am glad to be in on the search. One of these days he'll find what he's looking for and then, watch out! Sonny and them just might have to get their hats. Check him up close first chance you get!"

I must have left New York around the same time Coltrane was leaving Miles temporarily to spend the summer working with Thelonious Monk at the Five Spot Cafe downtown. Back in the midwest, I spent the summer washing dishes and bus-ing tables, following the music scene through the trade press and through first- and second-hand accounts provided by musicians who were fellow devotees. The grapevine was quivering with excitement.

I can only speculate that Monk and Trane must have loved one another musically. Listen to the way the pianist shouts his name—"Coltrane! Coltrane!"—on that old out-of-print Riverside LP *Monk's Music.* Monk, at the end of his solo on "Well You Needn't," pages Trane who takes up where his leader trails off, with an exhilarating statement that electrifies.

Certainly, Coltrane regarded the older musician with great admiration. "I would talk to Monk about musical problems," he later said, "and he would sit at the piano and show me the answers just by playing them." Among other things, Monk taught him the technique of sounding two to three notes on his horn simultaneously, a device which he subsequently put to delightful use in many of his exploratory solos.

Soon, however, Coltrane was back blowing and groping more daringly than ever with the re-formed Davis quintet, which, with some personnel changes and additions, was transformed into the remarkable sextet that brought him together with the alto saxophonist Cannonball Adderley and pianist Bill Evans to produce the classic *Kind of Blue* album that will doubtless sound as timeless and meaningful in a century as it does now and as it did in the late 1950s when it first made history.

1958 was the year Coltrane began to be widely talked about. He had by then become the most controversial new instrumentalist on the scene.

Time is funny. Coltrane was born in 1926 in Hamlet, North Carolina, son of a tailor who played music for fun, right around the time Louis Armstrong had come over to New York from Chicago and New Orleans and upset everybody once and for all. In his early twenties, following a hitch with the Navy band in Hawaii, he'd worked with such rhythm and blues stalwarts as Eddie "Clean Head" Vinson and Earl Bostic of my early school days. Before joining Miles, he had toured with Dizzy Gillespie and Johnny Hodges. Now in his thirties, Coltrane was new. It's important, I think, to mention here that, besides being ardent romantics, jazz enthusiasts are not unlike sports fans, journalists, academicians and theologians in their enduring love of controversy and the passionate discourse it generates.

Was Coltrane the new messiah or just another flashy, promising charlatan? Fifteen years previously, Charlie Parker had caught so many dutiful jazz eavesdroppers napping that fans, critics and active musicians alike were going out of their way almost comically to remain wakeful lest another elusive musical prophet sneak up on them unawares and unannounced.

"All you really gotta do," a trumpet-playing friend told me, "is to look at Tranes's initials. J.C. That oughtta tell you *something."*

But there were those people who were simply baffled or even irritated by what the man was playing. Many were outright hostile. All those showerings of sixteenth and thirty-second notes, those weird scales and modes, that polytonality— what the hell was it all supposed to mean?

"They can't dig Trane," my friend commented, "because he's too fast for them. They listen to him sounding all gentle on some ballad and think they've got him down. Then he'll turn around and double-time and triple-time 'em outta their minds. He's got too many things going on at the same time. He's too peculiar-sounding and unpredictable. You never know what kinda entrance he's gonna make. People get upset behind that. They wanna know is he for real or is he jiving? Now you don't mean to tell me Dizzy and Miles and Monk and them can't tell a good musician from a jive one?"

The jazz press of the day was hotly divided in its appraisal of his talent and significance. "Sheets of sound" was the term created by writer Ira Gitler to describe the overall effect that Coltrane's playing of that period achieved for him personally. The phrase, for better or worse, caught on. *Sheets of sound*, hmmm, that had an imaginative, perceptive ring to it. Maybe the man should be given the benefit of a doubt, and listened to more closely.

Comparisons between Coltrane's and Rollins' approaches to the tenor saxophone continued to be drawn until 1960 when Rollins went into self-imposed retirement for two years. It never seemed to matter that the two men were active contemporaries, each one respectful of the other's sound, style and capacity for inventiveness.

I found myself mistrustful of the assessments, pronouncements and exhortations of all the jazz commentators, professional and amateur, whose aim at core appears to have been to put this upstart newcomer in his place. And just where, if anywhere, was Coltrane's rightful place in the scheme of things? Obviously this was a matter that could only be settled in the hearts and aural imagination of individual listeners.

The overwhelming emotional and lyrical appeal of Coltrane's playing was clear to me from the moment he first invaded my world. I've never recovered from its strength, beauty and yea-saying exuberance, the same way I've never gotten over Coleman Hawkins.

Conveniently perhaps, the history of the music that's still called jazz is also a history of recorded performances. What a luxury it is to be able to fly around through time preserved as sound on record or tape. Re-entering such captured moments, it becomes increasingly difficult, if not impossible, to discern how much time itself transforms what I may actually hear. What was once shocking or disturbing to the ear might soon enough become acceptable, cherished or even hackneyed.

Recorded jazz is also the history of a process whereby

individual musicians, following the dictates of some secret ear, are forever casting their ideas upon winds that, all too often, blow those same creations back to them without benefit of copyright or royalties.

Coltrane was more fortunate than most in this respect. He didn't die penniless or washed up in anybody's poignant gutter. What's more, before he slipped out of the world he lived to see a lot of people change their ideas about his earlier performances, while he went on developing himself, extending and supplanting his own ideas about music at such a rapid rate that it was taxing for sympathetic fellow musicians (much less the public at large) to keep up with him.

I finally caught the Davis sextet live at Birdland in the summer of 1959. Two century-long years had passed in my life. Sure enough, there stood Coltrane, sounding totally different from the way he did on the latest recordings I'd gathered. It was the very night Miles Davis stepped outside between sets and got into an altercation with some cops about loitering. He had to be hospitalized. The band, winding up the evening without its leader, went on smoking and burning until the very air crackled with flames scorching enough to warm the heart of even a plainsclothes policeman. It was truly a Coltrane night. Mr. Talk hadn't been just talking.

I followed his music from then on until his sudden death in 1967, catching him live at every opportunity on both coasts.

I watched him pick up a whole new audience, a very broad-based one, when he picked up soprano saxophone and came out with "My Favorite Things" in 1960. I also watched him lose a few of those same puzzled fans when he showed up at the Jazz Workshop in San Francisco with altoist Eric Dolphy about a season later.

The Coltrane controversy resumed and never really subsided.

"Oh, that was terrible," he told Frank Kofsky in his last

interview, published in *Jazz & Pop*. "I couldn't believe it, you know, it just seemed so preposterous. It was so ridiculous, man... because they made it appear that we didn't even know the first thing about music.... And there we were really trying to push things off."

John Coltrane made no distinction between music, philosophy, religion and life. In his vision, they were all aspects of the same search for spiritual wholeness as his later recordings and comments attest. "I'm sure others will be a part of the music," he said in that final interview. "I know that there are bad forces put here that bring suffering to others and misery in the world, but I want to be the force which is truly for good."

Much has been said and witten about the Coltrane of the mid-1960s—a good deal of it reverential—but there were many Coltranes just as there are many musics that go to make up what is universally called jazz, better described as Afro-American classical music. A lifetime of listening has led me to believe that spirituals, blues, ragtime, New Orleans jazz, boogie-woogie, rhythm & blues, swing, bop and their derivatives are all indeed aspects of an enduring and self-regenerative musical tradition (or continuum, if you will) to which John William Coltrane has made lasting contributions.

He was glowing each time I met him, beginning with Berkeley in 1962 when he was visiting Wes Montgomery at the late Elton Mills' home (which was really a musicians' commune), and again the following year in a very wintry San Francisco. When I shook his hand and told him how reassuring it was for me and great many others to know that he was still here in the world, he simply smiled and looked beyond me shyly.

feels so good

CHUCK MANGIONE, 1978

It was one of those unscheduled deals where I found myself
with a whole day left over after working at a poetry festival
on Long Island. Exhausted from having expended all of the
physical, emotional and psychic energy that literary bashes
require, I decided to drive into Manhattan with a poet friend
and spend twenty-four hours doing as little as possible before
flying back West.

"Well," said my friend, "if you're only staying overnight,

I've got the key to an apartment upstairs from mine that this Columbia architecture student's vacated for the summer. It's quiet up there and you can rest up and sleep well."

It was quiet all right, by big city standards, but I barely got any of the sleep I needed. Like so many destinations in my New York world, this place was at the very top of a long, narrow, airless flight of stairs. Once I'd gotten past the inevitable web of key locks, fox locks, chain locks and *whew!*—the first sound to greet me as I stepped inside poured out of a table radio that was all aglow with the pop/disco hit of that feverish season: Chuck Mangione's "Feels So Good." By leaving the radio on and the lights hooked up to an automatic timer, the regular tenant sought to give the impression that the apartment was occupied. All the same, I kept thinking that if I were a sophisticated burglar scoping this joint—and there's no other kind of burglar in New York City—I would've known right away from the curtainless windows that somebody was running some kind of elaborate scam. But since it was anything but easy to get inside the building and the unit itself was up several tough flights, maybe my ghostly, absentee host had known what he was doing after all.

I wasn't feeling so good. Cruising into town across the George Washington Bridge had been almost as big a shock for me as the first time I'd subjected myself to a steambath when I'd been a teenager working the locker room and shoe-shine parlor at the Sidney Hill Health Club in downtown Detroit. This midsummer heat was like a solvent that, combined with the overpowering odor of uncollected garbage, turned me into compost long before I dragged my bags out of my friend's car to mount that brutal staircase.

In spite of the windows that were painted shut, and in spite of the sweat and grit pouring out of me, it still felt good in a queasy sort of way to be at liberty in a town that has always run me ragged. Not only didn't I have to call or call on anyone, but there was no threat of being interrupted, since only one person in town even knew where I was. The most pressing chore that lay before me was to pry open a couple of windows to get what I, being a naive Californian, believed would be a breath of air.

"The strangest things always happen to you in New York," my old friend Ann McIntosh used to say whenever I hit town. "Stuff that couldn't possibly happen to anybody else!"

I was thinking about this when I went for a late afternoon stroll along Duke Ellington Avenue. But what strange experience could possibly befall me this time? There was absolutely nothing doing, and I loved it. Deciding not to dine in a fancy Chinese-Cuban restaurant, I chowed down instead on pizza by the slice at some hole-in-the-wall where Barry Manilow's thumping "Copacabana," just released, kept the Puerto Rican counterman cranking up the volume on his radio, one of those big, booming, twin-speakered, proletarian specials specifically designed to induce apoplexy on buses and subways. No, this time in Manhattan I was determined to simply walk right in, sit right down and let my quiet mind roll on. Privately delighted at the prospect of having an absolutely uneventful time, I treated myself to some fresh fruit at a curbside produce stand, picked up the *Times* and strolled back home in a relatively hushed twilight that falsely promised a touch of breezy relief from the heat.

The minute I was back and settled at a desk in front of the tall, bare, front windows—equipped with pen and plenty of paper to begin doing what a writer does—my attention was drawn across the street at once to a window shade that was suddenly being yanked all the way up. In the window stood a man in nothing but briefs who then fell back upon an unmade double bed across which a young woman reclined. They appeared to be in their late twenties, perhaps early thirties, and both had mousey brown hair. The woman was wearing tennis shorts and a T-shirt.

In no time at all, while I tried to work, this couple had gotten the preliminary necking out of the way and were now about to get down, as the saying goes. Off came the clothes. I couldn't believe it. I also can't believe that I sat there in the full light of a glossy, hi-tech desk lamp and watched. Four stories down, kids were still playing in the street while people dawdled and chattered on crowded stoops, and thugs came and went. From where I sat, there were perhaps fifteen to twenty window scenes lit up before me, but in almost all of them, people were busy either watching or not watching their illuminated television screens. This one window alone had its own show going on, and it was undeniably x-rated. At first I felt embarrassed watching their performance, but as the evening wore on it gradually struck me that what this rabbity pair craved, possibly even more than sensual delight, was an audience.

Between couplings, the man would casually come to the window, still butt naked, and poke his tousled head outside to survey the siren world and catch his breath. Then he'd sit on the floor, remove papers from a briefcase, and begin to study them. He never got very far because the woman, ardently aroused—that is, hot to trot—would crawl to where he was plopped and, serpent-like, she'd begin tempting him again with nibbles and bites from her well-fruited garden. They must've carried on for hours on end, because at one point I doused my own light, took to bed, woke up to get a glass of water in the depths of night, looked across the way and saw that they were still at it.

As strange as it was to observe first-hand two human beings making passionate love, it was also unarousing and surprisingly, if not ridiculously, clinical. The experience made me realize how enormous a role personal involvment, emotion, anticipation and imagination play in giving the sex act its almost irrepressible power and titillating appeal. On that muggy night it became clear to me that sexual communion, however closely it might resemble a physical tournament, is anything but a spectator sport.

But the strangest leg of that incidental episode took

place the following morning, in broad daylight, when I descended to the street with my luggage to flag a taxi. Who should be emerging from the building across the street at that very moment but my uninhibited exhibitionists: he in his business suit with tortured briefcase in tow, and she in a crisp, proper summer office dress with her long hair pinned up. I might only have imagined this, but I could swear she glanced across the street at me with a lingering simper. And that's not all. The minute I settled in the cab and slammed the door, the cheerful driver snapped on his AM radio and there was Chuck Mangione and his brother Gap again, sending me off to the Eastside Airlines Terminal and back to California with "Feels So Good."

Like the pleasantly inoffensive breakfast aroma of steaming decaffeinated coffee with non-dairy creamer, Tang, scrambly powdered eggs, simulated bacon and two slices of hot-margarined Wonder Bread toast, the warm, polyunsaturated sound of Chuck Mangione's bronze record transported me through the rest of that morning, hatless and beardless, and on out into what remained of that American summer. Oh, the Bee Gees were "Staying Alive" and Bonnie Tyler was belting out "It's A Heartache," but somehow Chuck stuck, and everywhere I caught him grinning and hugging on that horn of his in a TV spot promoting the record, I couldn't help wondering what it must be like to make love to the world with all the lights turned on and the windows hoisted high.

gifts and messages

RAHSAAN ROLAND KIRK, 1965

Rahsaan's music is about as predictable as the rhythms of thunder breaking on a warm August night, or the evanescent shapes of falling snowflakes. It is solidly rooted in what he called Black Classical American tradition and yet it is always attractively new.

Consider the evening, years ago, when his quartet opened a set at San Francisco's now defunct Jazz Workshop with what was then a fresh, bossa-nova-flavored ballad called "The Shadow of Your Smile."

Soloing, Rahsaan descended from the stand and ambled through the audience, pausing at tables to permit one patron after another, just for the fun of it, to press a key on his tenor saxophone while he continued to blow. Working his way back toward the bar situated near the club's entrance, he lingered to slap hands with some latecomer and then—to the slow turning of heads—disappeared out the door. It didn't take long for most of us to realize that Rahsaan, with all of those exotic-looking instruments slung round his neck, had stepped out to stroll along Broadway, the avenue outside.

The rhythm section continued to cook and smoulder, taking, by turns, some memorable solos before Rahsaan reentered the Workshop, still playing beautifully and trailed by a queue of strung-out listeners picked up during his brief Pied Piper excursion. Head bobbing, horn cocked at the jauntiest of angles, he meandered right back up to the bandstand, never missing a beat, and topped things off with an unforgettable finale sounded simultaneously on manzello, strich and tenor sax.

The crowd went berserk.

light my fire

THE DOORS, 1967
JOSE FELICIANO, 1968

They were lighting fires like nobody's business then, and it wasn't all exactly what insurance investigators used to call Jewish Lightning. Early in the decade author James Baldwin, a resident of France, struck it big in America with a book that matched all his previous collections of essays for sheer intensity. Seemingly prophetic in the Biblical sense, Baldwin's perceptive volume, *The Fire Next Time*, hit home in its thoughtful and articulate assessment and indictment of American society at that urgent hour. Not long afterwards, television bombarded us with images of Watts on fire, Detroit on fire, Asian children being napalmed to a crisp in vivid, color footage that had nothing to do with the fancy footwork of James Brown and the Fabulous Flames.

And what a time that was! I used to get up mornings and pack, along with lunch, a very moist washcloth that I was careful to bag in plastic. I was enrolled at U.C. Berkeley where class attendance was increasingly becoming the last concern of students and professors. I should've been packing a hard hat as well, or, in any case, a helmet, but I seem to have been harried by other, more pressing concerns. You needed all this, that juicy rag and head protection. It was an everyday occurrence to be strolling across campus, not bothering anybody, passing through one of those jerry-rig scaffolded, construction passages when, all of a sudden, I might look up and see as many as a hundred people bolting toward me with policemen, sheriff's deputies or the National Guard in wicked pursuit, and—pshht!—I'd hear the pop of a tear gas cannister. This usually meant that there was just time enough to reach down into my brown bag lunch and retrieve that dripping washcloth, press it to my eyes, my nose, my mouth, then turn tail and haul ass all the way back to where I'd just come.

It was Third World Strike, it was People's Park, it was Free So-and-So, it was Vietnam blazing in the foreground, and it was one hell of a time to be going back to school! Dante assigned no circle in his Inferno to hypocrite revolutionaries, but I have no doubt that he would've done so had he run into some of the power-starved tricksters and buzzards who posed as radicals during that sadly trivialized epoch. It hurt, for example, to see so many minority-labeled freshmen flunk out under the dubious and thoughtless leadership of graduate students who organized the so-called Third World Strike at Cal. Most of these new undergraduates were on very special scholarships at this overwhelmingly white state university. What would you do if you picked up the phone one night to hear someone say: "Never mind who this is. This is a warning. You go to class tomorrow and it's all over for your ass! Got that?" And as if that weren't cruelty enough, I'd run into some of those mastermind rascals in the campus library nights where they would be diligently cramming and preparing for their own exams, papers, or theses.

One particularly eager and bloodthirsty self-styled campus militant let me know in no uncertain terms where aspiring artists such as myself stood in his particular political cult's scheme of justice: "Well, Al Young," he said. "You go on and keep writing your novels and poems and stories and shit. But after the revolution comes down, we intend to deal severely with niggers like you."

Who, I kept asking myself, was the Enemy? It wasn't until I had an important talk with Luis Monguió, an endearing Professor of Spanish and Latin American Literature at the University, and quite a compassionate man with a wry sense of humor, that I was made to understand where writers, artists and intellectuals stood with regard to belligerent politics and abrupt social change. Sr. Monguió, a Spaniard who had fought on the side that met with defeat in his troubled country's Civil War, explained how he had jettisoned a law career and come to America, where he took up literature. I had come to his office to discuss some translations I'd done of work by Nicolás Guillén, the great Cuban poet. After making some important and (to me) embarrassing minor corrections, Monguio encouraged me to continue translating and, more importantly, writing. Then he happened to glance out his office window at the campus scene below where scruffy students were preparing to do battle with the Blue Meanies, as those tear-gas and mace-wielding Alameda County Sheriff's Deputies were called because of the color of their uniforms. From my chair I too could see both sides psyching themselves up for what had become a daily scenario, complete with television news cameras to get it all down for posterity and the Six O'Clock News zombies.

"The Spanish Civil War," Monguió said, "taught me that, when it comes to bloody coups and revolts, artists and writers always have a choice. They can either choose to be lined up and shot by their enemies or by their friends. That's the way it always is. What you are doing and the degree you are working for will ultimately prove to be more important than all of this rhetoric about radicalism, revolution and the ghetto. And let us not forget to call these so-called ghettoes by their true name. You know as well as I do that they are slums. Slums! Those poor people, your people—they need what you have to offer."

Ever since Jack Kennedy got bumped in Dallas, the heat's been moving in. Now you can feel it coming from every direction in this corporate republic. People mean nothing; profits, everything. Even the time-honored precept of benign self-interest, like the proverbial baby with the bathwater, has been thrown out. The curtains have all but been drawn on an American era that once offered hope and promise to millions, to all but the miscolored anyway.

Back in those very sizzling Sixties, the sensational inter-planetary musician Sun Ra was saying: "The Man used to just be at a few people's door; now he's at everybody's door." Masses of middle-class Americans either don't know this yet, or don't care. Since the debacle and embarrassment of the Vietnam War, the country has been hiding its head in sands that continue to shift and blow out to uncertain seas ruled—crest, wave and bottom-line—by unimaginably powerful, multinational pirates who salute no flag and answer to no electorate except their own Boards of Directors whose members, as I once pointed out in a long poem, "do not operate under the influence of music." Like the erect male member in the popular saying, they have no conscience either.

Jim Morrison, singing leader of The Doors, was known as much for exposing himself on stage as for the music his group performed and the poetry he wrote. "Light My Fire." I can hear it now: the vaguely baroque-sounding intro on organ, the pounding drums, the banshee-squeal of electronic guitar, the steamy, bumptiously erected anapestic climax. Unngh!—there was, indeed, no time to hesitate or wallow in the mire. In those days, when everything had to happen now and all at once, and you weren't allowed to hold more than one opinion at a time. Later, Jose Feliciano—a blind, Puerto Rican-born marvel—covered that same hit with a mellow, leisurely version of his own; one that didn't so much burn as warm. The Doors were finally slammed shut. Feliciano, now sadly neglected, seems to have gotten locked into hard times, but he still jangles his musical keys.

Fire, of course, has always served as an incandescent metaphor for passion in poetry and song. That its image triumphed as the title of one of the hottest pop records in the declining years of the American Century seems to indicate something. I think it might have something to do with just how explosive and destructive the Empire has become.

chicken hawk's dream

AL YOUNG, 1968

Chicken Hawk stayed high pretty much all the time and he was nineteen years old limping down academic corridors trying to make it to twelfth grade.

Unlike his good sidekick Wine, whose big reason for putting up with school was to please his mother, Chicken Hawk just loved the public school system and all the advantages that came with it. He could go on boarding at home, didn't have to work, and could mess up over a whole year and not feel he'd lost anything.

He sat behind me in Homeroom Study Hall: sport shirt, creased pants, shiny black pointy-toed Stetsons, processed hair. He'd look around him on lean days and say, "Say, man, why don't you buy this joint off me so I can be straight for lunch, I'd really appreciate it."

One morning he showed up acting funnier than usual. Turns out he was half-stoned and half-drunk beause he'd smoked some dope when he got up that morning, then on the way to school he'd met up with Wine, so the two of them did up a fifth of Nature Boy, a brand of sweet wine well-known around Detroit. Wine wasn't called Wine for nothing. Between the Thunderbird and Nature Boy he didn't know what to do with himself. He was a jokey kind of lad who drank heavily as a matter of form—his form. "I like to juice on general principle," is the way he put it.

That morning Chicken Hawk eased up to me during a class break. "Man, I had this dream, the grooviest dream I had in a long time, you wanna know how it went?"

By that time I thought I could anticipate anything Chicken Hawk would come up with, but for him to relate a private dream was something else, something new. "What you dream, man?"

"Dreamed I was walkin around New York, you know, walkin round all the places where Bird walked and seen all the shit he seen and all through this dream I'm playin the background music to my own dream, dig, and it's on alto sax, man, and I'm cookin away somethin terrible and what surprise me is I can do the fingerin and all that jive—I can blow that horn, I know I can blow it in real life, I *know* I can! You know somebody got a horn I can borrow? I'll show everybody what I can do."

"Drew's got an alto and lives up the street from me. Maybe you could get your chops together on his horn. It don't belong to him, though. It's his brother's and Drew don't hardly touch it, he too busy woodsheddin his drums. I'll ask him if you can come over after school and play some."

"Aw, baby, yeah, nice, that's beautiful, Al, that sure would be beautiful if you could arrange all that. Think maybe Drew'd lemme borrow it for a few days?"

"Well, I don't know about all that, you could ask him."

"Yeah, unh-hunh, know what tune I wanna blow first? Listen to this . . ."—and he broke off into whistling something off a very old LP.

Wellsir—Drew said OK, to bring Chicken Hawk on over and we'd see what he could do. "But if you ask me the dude ain't nothin but another pothead with a lotta nerve. On the other hand he might just up and shake all of us up."

Six of us, mostly from band, went over to Drew's house after school to find out what Chicken hawk could do with a saxophone. As we went stomping through the snow, old Wine was passing the bottle—"Just a little taste, fellas, to brace ourself against the cold, dig it?"

Drew's mother, a gym teacher, took one look at us at the front door and said, "Now I know all you hoodlums is friendsa Drew's but you are not comin up here trackin mud all over my nice rugs, so go on round the back way and wipe your feet before you go down in the basement, and I mean wipe em good!"

We got down there where Drew had his drums set up and Drew got out his brother's old horn. "Be careful with it, Chicken Hawk, it ain't mine and Bruh gon need it when he get back from out the Service."

We all sat around to watch.

Chicken Hawk, tall, cool, took the horn and said, "Uh, show me how you hold this thing, just show me that, show me how you hold it and I'll do the rest."

"Show him how to hold it, Butter."

One of the reed players, a lightskinned fellow named Butter, leaned over Chicken Hawk and showed him where to place his fingers on the keys. Chicken Hawk looked at Butter as though he were insane. "Look here, gimme a little credit for knowin somethin about the thing, will you? You ain't got to treat me like I'm some little baby."

"Then go ahead and blow it, baby!"

"Damn, I shoulda turned on first, I'd do more better if I was high. Anybody got a joint they can lay on me?"

Everybody started getting mad and restless. Drew said, "Mister Chicken Hawk, sir, please blow somethin on the instrument and shut up!"

"Shit, you dudes don't think I can blow this thing but I'mo show you."

"Then kindly show us!"

Poor Chicken Hawk, he finally took a deep breath and huffed and puffed but not a sound could he make. "You sure this old raggedy horn work?"

"Don't worry about that, man, " Drew told him, "just go head and play somethin. You know—*play!*"

Chicken Hawk slobbered all over the mouthpiece and blew on it and worked the keys until we could all hear them clicking but still no sound. He wiped his lips on his coat sleeve and called his boy Wine over. "Now, Wine, you see me playin on this thing, don't you?"

"Yes, I am quite aware of that, C.H."

"You see me scufflin with it and it still don't make a sound?"

"Yes, I ain't heard anything, C.H., my man."

"Then, Wine, would you say—would you say just off hand that it could be that Drew's brother's horn ain't no damn good?"

Old Wine looked around the room at each of us and rubbed his hands together and grinned. "Well, uh, now I'd say it's a possiblility, but I don't know about that. Would you care for a little taste to loosen you up?"

Chicken Hawk screwed his face up, blew into the instrument and pumped keys until he turned colors but all that come out were some feeble little squeaks and pitiful honks. "Well, gentlemen," he announced, "I've had it with this axe. It don't work. It's too beat-up to work. It just ain't no more good.

I can blow it all right, O yeah—I could play music on it all right but how you expect me to get into anything on a jive horn?"

Drew took the saxophone and carefully packed it back inside its case. Wine passed Chicken Hawk the Nature Boy and we all started talking about something else. There were no jokes about what had just happened, no See-Now-What-I-Tell-You.

Drew got to showing us new things he'd worked out on drums for a rock dance he'd be playing that weekend. He loved to think up new beats. After everyone got absorbed in what Drew was doing, Chicken Hawk and Wine, well-juiced, eased quietly up the back steps.

I saw Chicken Hawk on 12th Street in Detroit. He was out of his mind, standing smack on the corner in the wind watching the light turn green, yellow, red, back to green, scratching his chin. He smiled at me.

"Hey, Chicken Hawk!"

"Hey now, what's goin on?"

"You got it."

"And don't I know it, I'm takin off for New York next week."

"What you gon do in New York?"

"See if I can get me a band together and cut some albums and stuff."

"Well—well, that's great, man, I hope you make it. Keep pushin."

"Gotta get my instruments out the pawnshop first, mmmm—you know how it is."

"Yeah, well, all right, take care yourself, man."

I did it my way

FRANK SINATRA, 1975

When the stout chapel organist sang this Paul Anka song over the public address system at my stepbrother Walter's funeral in Detroit, my beautiful Aunt Mae, whom I've loved since I was three, leaned over with tears in her eyes and whispered, "Well, they got that part right about Walter Junior, didn't they? The child really did do it his way."

Walter Simmons, Jr. was fair-skinned, butterscotch-colored, what people of color used to call light-complected.

He had woolly brown hair and light brown eyes, and he was also light-hearted, big-hearted and thin-skinned. Juju, as he'd been nicknamed from childhood by his slightly older sister Aveda, was so naturally generous that he would give you the hair off his head. All you had to do was ask. His father, my stepfather, died in his middle fifties when Juju was just entering his teens. My stepsister Aveda—whom I feel funny calling my stepsister since we were raised to accept one another full-bloodedly—had a knack for re-naming people. She was the one who came up with Mr. Toasty as an affectionate tag for Walter Simmons, Sr. Mr. Toasty had very little formal schooling, but he was a superbly talented and enterprising gambler and business man who had holdings in a restaurant known as The Green Hornet, several hotels, a fleet of delivery trucks and a couple of race horses, all of which he managed masterfully. Anyway, my sister's nicknames took. They took the way Lester Young's handles for his musician friends endured, for it was Lester—the President of the Tenor Saxophone, Prez—who put the monicker of Sweets on trumpeter Harry Edison, affixed the titular Sir to pianist Charles Thompson's name, and who personally pinned, like a flower, the fragrant sobriquet of Lady Day on Billie Holiday.

Walter Junior, Juju, by any other name you called him, was brilliant. I tend to remember him most as a kid because by the time he'd turned seven I was packing all the books and records in my attic room to leave for college. The kid was able recall anything that he'd seen, heard or read in feckless detail. He was blessed with the kind of photographic memory that I intuitively attributed to a character named Shakes in my first novel, *Snakes*. Even after he became addicted to heroin, Juju maintained a high grade average as a business major at Wayne State University before he dropped out. He took an accounting job in a bank. Goodly sums of cash began to disappear and even though the bank was never able to determine exactly how money was being siphoned from its computer-controlled supply, my mother and others put two and two together. Juju was fired.

The house began to be burglarized. My mother didn't care to press charges. Long, distressing phone conversations between California and Michigan darken my memories of those intervening years. Finally, Juju was banned from the house. He drifted into a hand-to-mouth—or ought I say hand-to-vein—existence. Like all of his addict friends, if you could call them friends, he lived only to get high. Aveda, whom he loved and in whom he confided to the end, told me that there would be times when he would find himself resurrected from a near overdose and say, "Sis, I almost got away from here that time! Oh well, maybe next time."

What must be mentioned is that Detroit was probably the key heroin capital of the continental United States in those days. The stuff was everywhere: in the streets, in the schools, on the playground, in the auto plants, the suburbs, at universities—everywhere! The one-time head of Detroit's Narcotics Squad allegedly resigned from the Police Department to work for the other side. He then went on to become one of the richest dope dealers in the Middle West. In a sense I suppose you could say that Juju was simply following out the normal peer patterns of his times.

But what was wrong? Years later I'm still trying to piece it all together, and it remains too painful a subject to range over at length. During rare visits home I would try to talk to Juju, but he would either be too stoned or cleverly evasive. He was proud of his oldest brother who was writing books, even to the point of introducing me to some of his pals who had all read *Snakes* and loved the way it seemed to speak directly to them and their immediate everyday problems. There's a character in the book named Champ who gets strung out on skag, but who is careful to warn his younger buddies not to follow along in his dumb footsteps. "You really got the whole thing down, man," one of them told me. "We passed that book around until the pages got raggedy and started falling out!" But these young men seemed helpless to help themselves.

Juju gradually enlisted in a methadone maintenance program. I've always had mixed feelings about this alternative since it seems to prolong and foster a dependence on drugs. Heroin itself was developed as a cure for opium and morphine addiction which was practically epidemic in America in the early 1900s, the heyday of patent medicines and elixirs. So here we were, doomed again. Besides, Henry Ford had long ago dismissed history as "bunk." Methadone went on the black market. To hear Juju and Aveda tell it, even the social workers who were supposed to be administrating these so-called maintenance programs, even *they* were sampling their own cure and nodding out over desks right there on the job.

Just when Juju seemed to be making some delicate semblance of progress, he got it into his head somewhere in 1974 to take an unloaded pistol into a Big Boy burger joint and pull a stick-up. Within minutes, squadrons of Detroit's Finest were on their way to haul him off. A first-time offender, he got six months to a year at Jackson State Penitentiary. To no one's surprise, he was a model prisoner, and was paroled after serving six months. Out on good behavior, he fell back into his old habits, violated parole and in no time at all was back in the slam. Like Jimmy Reed sings in one of his jump blues, Juju told Mother, "You better take out some insurance on me." She never did.

He was found dead in his cell one morning during a routine wake-up call. From what I've been able to piece together, Juju must have been surreptitiously injecting himself in the joint. Aveda remembers the last visit he'd paid to her, shortly before he was locked up again, when he was rheumy of eye and jaundiced-looking. The autopsy report cited serum hepatitis as the cause of death. Again, I can only speculate, but it seems reasonable to presume that Juju, probably knowing that he was infected, possibly through the use of unclean needles, deliberately avoided revealing his condition to prison health authorities. And the question circles my mind again and again: How badly did he truly want to slip out of this vulnerable cocoon of flesh?

At the funeral service, I spoke briefly about how Walter Junior had never felt loved. What I couldn't say and can only halfway say now is that something happened to Juju after his father died. He felt betrayed and, in many ways, blamed the world, for which he saw no hope, certainly not for Black people; and he blamed our mother. The year before, I had flown home to help bury my father, a victim of cancer, and now I was back to bury my brother, barely 25, a victim of another kind of unbenign growth, and of his own persistent and self-destructive brilliance. For him the body must have seemed like a painful and troublesome encumbrance, like bandaging, like a shroud, like a burden the mind thinks it no longer needs in its clumsy, insatiable hunger for nothing less than total, ineffable bliss.

goodbye
porkpie hat

CHARLES MINGUS, 1959
JEFF BECK, 1975
JONI MITCHELL, 1979

Yes, that was sadness you saw shining out of Lester's lidded eyes upturned beneath that porkpie hat; but what manner of sadness?

Was it the sadness of New Orleans trumpet legend King Oliver in his December years where we find him selling fruit and vegetables from a roadside truck for a living? Could it be anything like the bittersweet sadness of the overlooked bop arranger and pianist Tadd Dameron dialing "B for Beauty" on an old French telephone at Fontainbleu, who early abandoned a medical career because he thought the world was sorely in need of beauty? And what about the sumptuous sadness of Coleman Hawkins, inventor of jazz saxophone, and colorist and shaper of horn poems?

No, the sadness you heard was Lester's alone. Charles Mingus captured it in "Goodbye Porkpie Hat," Jeff Beck picked up on it, and Joni Mitchell recites and recounts it as best she can in mere words. But Lester, of course, is himself the source: a musical force that gave the world so much loving sound that it still hurts to play his final recordings or to remember how pitifully wasted he was during those declining Jazz At The Philharmonic concert years when much of his exuberance and genius had fled him, when everything that he had to say on his horn souded like variations on sighs of resignation. Whatever became of all that wondrous discourse that used to pour and trickle and skeet out of him like light from some heavenly reservoir? New Orleans? Kansas City? New York? The world? Like youthful fame and stamina, the past must have seemed a dream to him as he willfully let himself go.

Prez, the President, who never campaigned for any office, was resigned by then as only genius can be resigned. Weary of telling his story this way and that, night after night, flight upon flight; climbing, descending, he was ready to step aside and do his brooding in private.

His eyes were sad with gin and what it drowns. We fish who swam his ocean keep him young. I used to lie and say he was a distant cousin, but it was true.

*would you like
to know a secret?*

THE BEATLES, 1965

There used to be a little band under the Corona beer-built bandshell on the beach at Lake Chapala that featured a good local quartet—three young men and a lovely girl—that sang to beat the band. It seems they had a weakness for Beatles tunes, and they used to play the hell out of this one late every afternoon. Now I know that might sound peculiar, but that's just how it played. Think about it: Mexicans crooning and shouting songs written by Englishmen who got their juice from a musical idiom that is fundamentally Afro-American.

I used to sit there with beautiful Tissa, all of sixteen, and her mother Edith, who were letting me share their house, and I would think about that stuff. Sometimes a local youth named Umberto Anaya would join us. For me, Umberto was one native son with roots everywhere. Footholds anyway.

Umberto knew the women who sat all day long in the tortilleria, flattening and smacking dough, working the wheels and ovens. He knew the street vendors, the restaurateurs, bankers, druggists, mechanics, taxi drivers, the policía—and quickly distinguished the local cops from the moonlighting mercenaries who filed into Chapala from nearby Guadalajara and Mexico City weekends to bust speeding tourists in their ostentatious cars. Foreigners and countrymen, these jokers ticketed them all. Mordelones is what they were called. That's because the idea was to put the bite on the offender; to bite off a bit of that holiday cash for themselves. And, lest you misunderstand, they would leave bleeding teethmarks in your suntanned behind.

Umberto knew all the beggars and drunks, the old men—indigenous and tourist—who sunned and stumbled around the zócalo all day long. He knew who owned what and how much power that entitled them to. In fact, Umberto had a brother whom everybody called El Azteca—because he claimed to be of pure Aztec ancestry—but whose real name was Alfonso. Alfonso knew a little something about ownership and power too; he was in real estate.

Chapala was Umberto's; it was home and it was him, and I can't tell you how comforting it can be to be on amicable terms with a true native when you're residing, however insecurely, on foreign soil. But, then again, Umberto made a special point of getting acquainted with all the Yanks and Canadians, Europeans and Aussies who straggled in and out of this peculiar little Jaliscan community with its large Mexican upper class and middle class, its American Legion, its legion of resident Texans, golfers, elderly lady gadabouts and elegantly frayed bag-women; pensioners down from Colorado Springs, Sioux Falls and Cleveland who had dreamed through many a crisis back home of finally retiring to the land of Mañana where everything under the Coppertone sun costs under a buck; where it seemed as if happiness could be had for a song, maybe for just a dance, even if you had no particular sense of rhythm and didn't even know how to carry your decimal, much less a tune. Hell, even oldtime leftwingers from the States who knew all about *imperialismo* and United Fruit Company's banana republics—even they would slip down to take in Acapulco or the then still habitable Puerta Vallarta from time to time.

At twenty-three, Umberto seemed to have seen and heard it all. He made his rounds and kept his eyes open. When it came to drumming up prospects, he didn't sit around waiting for Opportunity to knock. With Umberto, chances were good that he would've already spotted Opportunity waddling up the block, long before Opportunity set foot on his doorstep.

That spring a famous folksinger—as alluring as she was radical—hit town. She sang the language, even spoke it some, and in no time at all she and Umberto were clicking like a pair of crisp castanets. In a sense, I suppose you could say that she took him under her spiritual wing. They hit it off real *simpático,* and for a spell became the talk of the town. The dark young celebrity with flashing eyes was, in fact, so taken with Umberto that she offered him a trip north, to Northern California where she lived, with funding, schooling, affection and her encouragement thrown into the bargain. But she had to be on her way. There were gigs, tours, interviews, recording dates back home and abroad.

She left Umberto with thoughts swimming around in his head the way scrumptious whitefish navigate the depths of Lake Chapala. Every day that we hung out together, Umberto, who was handsome and dreamy, seemed to grow ever more dazed at the prospect of traveling to the States.

"Ah, you know," he'd say to me, "one day I am taking that trip to California, but not today, not today, no, not yet. There is still so much that I must do here, so much. But tonight, we party. We go to Ajijic and party and dance with the girls and drink and make music."

He dreamed, O he dreamed, for I used to wonder what manner of dreaming went on in back of those shiny black eyes: eyes so simple and at the same time so complex that I could tell that Umberto was also looking for something far beyond himself and the immediately tangible, pulsating world. But he would ask me about the U.S., about California, about how it felt to travel and visit other lands. I envied his rootedness; he envied my mobility. Somehow I couldn't picture him settling anyplace but in Chapala, just as I knew that belonging to a town rather than to the world would always stifle my own native spirit.

And what was I? Nothing but a poet and storyteller approaching his mid-twenties who played guitar, sang, and studied cities, towns, open spaces, the seasons, the heavens, oceans, human speech, metaphysics, contemporary mythology, folklore, solitude, passionate loneliness, states of mind, the sounds of the world, love and its distances, and the colors and configurations of suffering and soulful jubilation. Working at crazy jobs to buy myself time, I used whatever leftover or borrowed money I came by to explore unfamiliar territories that lay both within and outside myself. At the time of my arrival in Chapala from Guadalajara that spring, I was only beginning to learn that matter itself was a manifestation of spirit. In brief, I was what I've always been: a survivor enchanted by the sanctity of bodies and soul.

The very first afternoon in town I looked up Edith Eddy. I say "looked up" and yet all I had was her name which had been jotted on a raggedy scrap of paper by Charles Washington, a pal of her husband, Rusty Eddy, back in Monterey. "I don't have an address," Charles had told me, "but I'm sure if you just turn up in town and ask, somebody'll know where to find her." And sure enough, two thousand miles later, I abandoned my room in Guad, rolled into Chapala, and fresh off the bus asked the first person I spotted in the center of town. He didn't know Edith, but a sandy-haired, gypsy-looking American woman, who happened to be strolling past—trailed by half a dozen part-Mexican kids—overheard. Sullen and nosey, yet eager to help, she directed a taxi driver straight to the Eddys' door.

They lived in an old house built of gentle warm gray stones piled and mortared atop one another, surrounded by a toppling, low stone fence. I was taken right away by this solid rock villa with its red brick-colored tile roof set off from the narrow dirt road by vivid clusters of tropical trees and flowering plants. Not knowing where the front door was, I tapped at a window while the cabbie waited. A pretty, tan girl with sea-tinted eyes and lustrous hair that fell to her waist, stuck her head out the window and, smiling inquisitively, said, "*Sí, señor.*" We carried on in Spanish, which she spoke liltingly with no trace of an accent, and in that roundabout Hispanic way established that this was, indeed, the right place and, yes, she would go get her mama.

And that was how it went. I moved right in with Edith, Tissa and the two younger boys, Roger and Glenn. They were all there taking a year-long breather from their home in Pacific Grove, California, where father and husband Rusty Eddy was going through some manner of emotional crisis. After that I blended right into the life around there so that meeting Umberto, his brother Alfonso, Afro-American painter-in-exile Arthur Monroe and all the others scattered from Chapala to Jocotepec who were grappling with life in imaginative ways— well, it was only a matter of course.

Of all things, that early Beatles tune brings it all back, makes it easy to remember what it was like to suddenly show up like some character in a story yet to be written by Mexican authors Juan Rulfo or Octavio Paz. The sky now seems always to have been blue turning green. Little children ran up and down the dusty roads. Burros hee-hawed at dawn like roosters to welcome an unbelievably red, unpeeled orange of a sun. You could smell the lake just down the road, even though the fragrant barriers of bougainvillea, bamboo, coconut, lemon and palm trees made it seem a thousand walkable miles away. Around the bend from my borrowed lodgings, there was always a man selling *cocolotes,* drinking coconuts, or someone hustling watermelon in the shade on a hot day, and all you had to do was dig down in your pocket, plunk your money down and sit on the ground under a tree older than both my great-great grandfathers and bite into melon meat and spit out the seeds; tuned in totally to the rhythm of the world as it tick-tocked in your blood, and knowing in your heart like you did as a kid that the word *bourgeois* secretly meant bullshit.

It was all so simple and yet so complicated and unapproachable that, unbeknownst to buddies like Umberto, I'd sit on a bench down by the lake, long after the fishermen had hauled in their nets, and study the moon. After quietly nutting out this way, I would then go home and orchestrate poems or, worse, scribble exuberant, raw prose that seemed at the time to frame a way of experiencing the transitory world; of being in that world yet not strictly of it, a world that is still rapidly losing ground to technocratic fascism and to the horrors posed by hunger on the one hand, and heartless greed on the other. Even then I was painfully aware that total biological control is the impending, all-around global goal.

Now you know at least one of my secrets.

You also doubtless know what became of the Beatles.

Edith, tall, radiant and splendidly white-haired—that big-hearted woman who had grown up in Ceylon with her two sisters, speaking German, French and English—in time left her Spanish behind and returned to California to continue caring for Rusty, her sensitive, flamboyant philosopher of a husband who gradually lost his eyesight before moving himself down to Mexico, where he ultimately and stoically took his own life. Like me, and like we all were then, she's still poor and working, getting up every morning to punch in at 5:30 a.m. But she still laughs a lot and her eyes still sparkle. She loves life. She loves people. She loves her kids but doesn't live for them.

The last I heard, Tissa, ever the free spirit with little interest in either bearing or rearing children, had gone from being a New York fashion model to film work and traveling around England with rock bands to becoming involved with the art of dressage, and holding down a waitress job in Marin County to support herself and her passion for horses. Roger's a guitarist now. He was co-founder of a band called California, then formed his own Los Angeles-based group, played with the Mark Slocum Band in Sun Valley and then went on to devote himself to the struggle of making a name for himself in the music business. Glenn, the youngest, became a classical dancer, working first with a New York troupe, and then with a company in the Netherlands.

Alfonso Anaya, the Aztec, is probably a peso millionaire in Chapala by now; an avid real estate developer and a stolid, though eccentric, member of the Mexican Rotarians. His younger brother Umberto finally got to the States where he spent a few weeks visiting his folksinger sponsor and other friends on the West Coast. But it didn't take him long to realize where he felt most at home. I wonder if he ever thinks about his pal Alberto, the writer, the one who used to haul out his guitar and sing Mexican, Puerto Rican, Afro-Cuban, South American and Spanish songs enticingly enough to draw people down to the lake where we had all those memorable impromptu parties? Hey, Umberto, forget about that money you never paid me back! This memory of our warm camaraderie is enough.

Charles Washington moved to England, bought a house in Nottingham and for years has been producing Caribbean programs for the B.B.C. and working for the London Planning Council.

Me, I'm still here, still struggling, still on earth; except now I have a lovely, rare wife and a child of my own: a son who's growing like a bamboo shoot and who takes delight in reading, storytelling, writing, soccer, basketball, baseball, swimming, camping trips and playing the piano. I love what I do and what, by chance, it happens to make happen.

And from what they tell me, Lake Chapala and the town that it frames so dramatically—both are flourishing and going on about their business.

if I had wings like noah's dove

AL YOUNG *LIVE*, 1964

It was my grandmother—Mrs. Lillian Campbell of Pachuta, Mississippi—who passed down to me the first folk songs I ever learned, and they were mostly old Negro spirituals along the order of "Steal Away," "Meetin' at the Buildin'," "Didn't My Lord Deliver Daniel," and "Pharoah's Army." There seemed to be hundreds of them that she would half-sing and half-hum in the classic fashion that musicologists have learned to call "moaning." Morning, noon and nighttime, from dawn to dark, one song would turn into another or back into itself as Mama drew water from the well, washed, milked, cooked, swept, scrubbed, gardened, quilted, sewed, doctored, scolded, and wrung the necks of chickens. Often I would study her at the kitchen woodstove, getting up a big iron pot of something for early-afternoon dinner and moaning to herself while she smiled out the window at fig trees or at a particular red bird. Music was merely one of her ways of getting through days.

We didn't have electricity, running water, gas or a car; nor did we have any idea that what we sang or listened to was American folk music.

At the age of seven, I made up my own folk song in the manner of Hank Williams who was knocking everybody down out there by then with his "Hey, Goodlookin'," and "Move It Over." Mama would crack up when I sat out in the porch swing with my little cigar box guitar and whined:

O Hopalong Cass'dy
You treated me nasty
when I was in Texas, Tennessee....

I wanted to grow up and be a cowboy. Like all the other boys my age, I wanted to go galloping across plains giving crooks the uppercut, the same as Tex Ritter, Gene Autry, Roy Rogers and all the others; hammering out a tune by the camp-fire nights, and just generally being It. It was Mama who put the facts to me one rainy afternoon when Cousin Jesse and I were lollygagging around the woodpile by the fireplace, polishing up our cap pistols, tickled that it was too wet to be out in the field picking cotton.

"Boys, y'all ever heard tell of a colored cowboy? You ever seen one at the picture show or in a funnybook?"

Of course, we hadn't. There was nothing out on the Negro cowboys at that time, although I was later to learn how many of them there had actually been. That was one dream I had to gradually let go.

But I hung onto the music as it went charging through

my blood in the form of gospel, folk song, blues, country & western, rhythm & blues, pop, bebop, cool, modern, classical, international—and then came the first fun chord I learned to strum on a real guitar. Suddenly I was back into folk.

By then, I'd become a freshman at the University of Michigan, Ann Arbor, and the Cold War was massacring hearts and minds. A few days after I moved into South Quad, the resident House Mother had me to lunch, along with the roommate they'd placed me with. His name was Bill McAdoo and he was older; a workingclass political firebrand from Detroit. Bill's mother was Jewish and his father Black. At one point during our simple repast of mash potatoes, shiny gravy, tinned peas and something called City Chicken, our blue-haired Dorm Mother squinted across the table. "I'll have you boys know," she glowered and announced, "that we believe in taking regular showers and baths around here."

At the end of that first semester, I flew the coop. I moved out of all dormitories into the world at large where the living was never easy, but where at least there was room to breathe. Not having been raised white, Republican or middle class, I had no recourse but to go my own way, and I've been going my own way ever since. If you were different in those days, you were automatically slap-sticker-labeled Communist, or Red or Pinko at worst, and Beatnik at best. I was never even either. I'd done a lot and read a lot—or so I thought—but, leery of schools, I was starving for lasting knowledge, spiritual growth and stimulating friendship. Classes weren't enough somehow. Fraternities seemed both fatuous and stifling. And all the beautiful girls of the colored aristocracy were busy planning their coming-out parties or sensibly stalking their own kind—boys from good backgrounds with good hair and lucrative futures. Not much had changed since earlier days at Hutchins Intermediate in Detroit when I sat backstage with Mary Jean Tomlin, later to become Lily, at some school show in which we were both performing, speculating about what became of talented kids who didn't come from privileged families.

In college I gravitated toward activities germane to my natural interests, and toward people who, like myself, remained open to experience. So it wasn't surprising to find myself taking up with budding writers, poets, playwrights, dreamers, journalists, intellectual mavericks, politicos, painters, sculptors, photographers, actors, hipsters, renegades, math visionaries, townies, composers; all manner of self-invented misfits, including, of course, musicians.

Music soothed. Music helped. Music helped soothe the loneliness and my sense of uncertainty, just as it eased the sting and nagging strain of color prejudice, social awkwardness, McCarthy Era paranoia and the all-around savagery of blooming adolescence itself; a beastly climbing rosebush with thorns no more imaginary than the wounds they open. Red with passion and hopelessly romantic, it eventually took a witty professor of Spanish to thoughtfully point out that the writers who were *románticos* by and large lived very short lives (1803-1836) whereas the classicists tended to have gravestones that read 1795-1889. As it had done for my grandmother, music still got me through days.

Occasionally I would sit up all night by myself, grave, determined not to turn in before I had mastered some difficult Leadbelly lick or learned the changes to something Sonny Terry and Brownie McGhee had recorded. I was learning stuff from everybody: Blind Willie Johnson, Snooks Eaglin, Reverend Gary Davis, chain-gang prisoners taped by Alan Lomax at Mississippi State Penitentiary (Parchman Farm), Odetta, Blind Blake, Woody Guthrie, Mississippi John Hurt, Lonnie Johnson, Elizabeth Cotten, John Lee Hooker, Robert Johnson, Bascom Lunsford, Jean Ritchie, Pete Seeger, The Weavers, Josh White, Big Bill Broonzy, Muddy Waters, Howlin' Wolf, Bo Diddley, Harry Belafonte, Len Chandler, Cynthia Gooding, Jesse Fuller, Theodore Bikel, Sister Rosetta Tharpe, The Staple Singers, Lightin' Hopkins, Charles Mingus, Ray Charles, and from sources all around me.

All of it was "ethnic" as far as I was concerned. I mean, I

took the late Bill Broonzy's word for it when he made that remark of his that went: "Anything a man can play is folk music; you don't hear no dogs or cats or horses singing it, do you?" At the time I wasn't aware that Louis Armstrong had said something similar long before that. I was hung up for a spell on quite a few backwoodsmen and citybillies, to say nothing of all those meditative foreigners with their thumb pianos, bouzoukis, balalaikas and sitars.

As I came upon other amateurs given to similar habits, we would work out songs, tunes and pieces and get together regularly to swap material and techniques as well as show off our fragile accomplishments. These get-togethers, when they weren't strictly for fun, were called hoots, and hoots were serious and very big at college.

If a hootenanny was jubilant enough, you were apt to hear English majors doing field hollers; pre-meds having a go at lumberjack songs; students of library science singing about robbing banks and hopping freight trains; business administration people getting all wrapped up in "Hallelujah, I'm a Bum"; eighth-generation Yanks armed with banjos, fiddles and mandolins, sounding more like Confederates than Flatt & Scruggs and the Foggy Mountain Boys; future ballistics missile experts working up a sweat on "Ain't Gonna Study War No More"; kids reared in traffic jams reminiscing about "The Old Cotton Fields Back Home."

There were doctrinaire folkniks who took themselves and their image quite seriously. I can see now how, in many ways, they helped usher in the great costume phenomenon that would overtake the Western World by the time the Sixties ended. Personally, I had grown weary of workshirts, neckerchiefs, buckskin coats, clunky boots, railroad caps, peasant dresses and blouses, cowboy hats, Levi suits, leather vests, Paul Bunyan shirts and thrift shop resurrections long before that overly studied mode of dress gave way to Jesus gowns, capes, plumage, Shakespearian garb, Salvation Army bandleader coats, paratrooper gear, dashikis, Cossack uniforms, Mao jackets, coolie togs, aviator helmetry, sharecropper bibs and sundry Me-Tarzan-You-Jane getups.

At length, I came to perform; sometimes around town as a single and other times with well-rehearsed string combos such as those formed variously with the likes of Marc Silber, Perry Lederman, Bernie Krause, Joe Dassin and Felix Pappalardi. Marc became a guitar maker and opened—first in New York and then in Berkeley—a shop called Fretted Instruments. Perry hooked up with Indian sarodist Ali Akhbar Khan and became immersed in ragas and a personal mysticism. Bernie went on replace Eric Darling in the Weavers and later teamed with fellow synthesist Fred Beaver to form Beaver and Krause, a pioneering fusion repertory unit. Joe Dassin, son of film director Jules Dassin, returned to France where he became a pop music idol before suffering a fatal heart attack in Tahiti in 1980. As for Felix Pappalardi, the only bona fide conservatory trainee among us—who was equally at home on guitar, bass, fiddle and trumpet—he launched the rock band Cream, became an international success and remained highly visible and respected as a player, arranger and producer on the New York music scene.

Show business was something I could never hack, not on any sustained basis. It got to the point where it felt too much like jail. It also didn't seem to matter where I worked—the Midwest, the East, the West Coast. I took care of business on the gig; I always delivered. The money, especially at college, paid for rent, food, clothing, free time, and also kept my digs overrun with staples such as books, records, tape and beer. But then I would catch glimpses of myself, a captive on the stand or on stage all those professional nights when I would've been happier writing or reading or—rather than merely singing about it—actually be out walking with my baby down by the San Francisco Bay.

Perhaps I did become, after all, that singing cowboy my grandmother lovingly discouraged. Then again, for all I know, I might very well still be in show biz. But I've changed my axe and I've changed my act, and the changes never seem to stop coming.

big noise
from winnetka

BOB HAGGART / RAY BAUDUC, 1937

I started whistling just as soon as I found out I could do it at the age of six. The family was living in Detroit at 5631 Roosevelt Street, an upstairs flat where, to pass the time, my younger brothers and I would chase rats or sit in front of the coal furnace and make up radio shows while we pictured the action taking place in the flames before us. In addition to ad-libbing dialogue, we would sing and clap out the theme songs and background music to these programs, improvising as we went along but mostly borrowing melodies picked up from recordings our dad played practically non-stop when he was at home.

My father, newly and honorably discharged from the Navy, had taken a job on the assembly line at the Chevrolet plant where he was to work until his death by cancer almost thirty years later. Prior to his service days, he played tuba and baritone horn with a colored band that traveled and even played on the radio Saturday afternoons in Laurel, Mississippi. We had moved to Michigan from Ocean Springs, my coastal Mississippi birthplace, where we'd lived in a little house whose layout I can still remember perfectly, just as I've never forgotten the voices of White Folks inside our large wooden Zenith radio barking about the Gnat-zees and the Dirty Japs. And, ah, the warmth I felt on those nights when the whole family would be sprawled around the same room, tuning in the big band broadcasts from up north that featured live pickups of Duke Ellington, Count Basie, Charlie Barnet, Artie Shaw, Jimmy Lunceford, Woody Herman and all the famous Swing Kings of the 1940s.

Thank God it was through music that I first became acquainted with the breadth and quirkiness of the outside world.

I heard my father whistling all the time, so I began to practice it myself. Soon after we reached Detroit, he heard me doing it and said, "Where'd you learn to make all that racket, boy?"

"Just figured it out, I guess."

"Well," he laughed. "I reckon you know you're on your own now."

And on my own I took whistling out into the streets and alleys and roads and fields of my wayward life. The sheer pleasure and simplicity of it brings such delight that I'm disheartened by the gradual but certain disappearance of this pastime from the world. I suppose it's a bit like singing or humming to oneself. You don't hear much of that either anymore. There was a time, for example, and not so long ago, when families and friends clustered on stoops or front porches and sang, either a cappella or to guitar or harmonica accompaniment. Like social or semi-private storytelling, that gentle form of relaxation and sharing has mostly gone the way of Amateur Night at the local movie house or going for walks on summer nights in cities for the sheer fun of it. Everything now is tightly organized and geared to the Dow-Jones Index. Not only that, but everyone's opting for stardom. It just won't do to be caught whistling without any prospect of landing a record contract or, in any event, a Special on CBS.

I still whistle when I walk because it's fun, but also because it helps me clear my mind. Sometimes, though, I catch myself whistling because the world is too much with me, too much to bear, and I need to be out of it for awhile. Music provides the perfect exit.

It's like this: I got the blues in Mexico City one night, way over there back behind the Zócalo, and there was nothing else to do but hit the pavement, purse my lips and whistle my way back towards home. Home at the time was an airless hotel I was flopping at in the workingclass Roma District. Living on vitamin pills and nerve, I was lonely and homesick, caught up in that incendiary solitude that prolonged isolation abroad can spark. The surest way I knew to soothe myself was to do some brisk walking for a few miles whistling and singing as much as I could. I was bending notes I'd never known could be bent. And you should have seen the people getting out of my way who figured me crazy, the same as the people back home. Can you imagine that? And all I was doing was whistling the blues.

My favorite whistling days don't come from those instances when people, usually people older than myself, stop me to say, "My, that sounds good! You must be happy!" No, the biggest kick I get is when little children pause to listen and reveal their feelings by puckering up and having a go at it themselves.

confirmation

CHARLIE PARKER, COMPOSER

Dear Bird,

It's been much too long, hasn't it? I've written you a few poems, whistled you on streets, practiced your licks on piano and sung you in showers and autos all over the world for most of my years. You got away from here before I ever got a chance to say my hellos in person, but I've been doing what I can to spread the spirit of your music around, and to try and get people—especially people of the sub-Saharan diaspora, shall we say—to recall what your music taught us; to remember that we're free.

Hey, let me tell you, it hasn't been easy. Most sub-Americans don't even know who you are or what you did. But some white people do. It's funny sometimes. Your presence persists. Just now when I sat to title this letter for the book I'm writing, it took forever to come up with "Confirmation." But as soon as I did, I flipped the radio on that I keep beside my typewriter and there was your music, the very song, "Confirmation," coming right at me from Manhattan Transfer, a singing group that's put nice lyrics to your rollercoaster melody. The moment it occurred, I smiled because the same thing's happened when I've been either writing or strongly thinking about Charles Mingus. I was so touched, in fact, that I rang up my pal Betty McGettigan—the one who's completing Duke's unfinished opera, *Queenie Pie: La Plus Belle.* Betty laughed and told me that she has been enjoying the identical experience. There's a lot of speculation we could get into here, but that isn't the reason I'm writing.

Bird, you must know that for a long time now I've toyed with the idea of writing a screenplay about you and your life. Of course, Lester Young would be in there, Fats Navarro, Dizzy Gillespie, Miles Davis, Thelonious Monk, Bud Powell, Kenny Clarke, Jay McShann, Sarah Vaughan, Earl Fatha Hines and so on. The big trick, as I envisioned the project, would be getting it casted properly. For such a picture to work, we'd have to find the right stars to play you guys. That's why I always figured that Dizzy would have to be played by John Belushi, and Monk by Dan Aykroyd. Ringo Starr would make a perfect Max Roach, don't you think? And nobody but George Carlin could do Lester justice. Mick Jagger would make the perfect Bud Powell to a Mingus played by Peter Ustinov. Can't you also see David Niven as an older, seasoned Kenny Clarke, and Robert DeNiro as the youthful Fats Navarro? Don't know about you, but I rather favor this woman named Deborah Harry for Sarah's role. She heads up a group called Blondie? I caught that band in London, long before they broke big in the States, and even then I thought she'd be just right for the part, although we might have to dub in Sarah's voice and have Deborah do a lip-synch.

As for you, Bird, I can think of no more appropriate actor to portray Charles Christopher Parker than Omar Sharif. That's right, Omar Sharif. Why? Because Omar is vaguely Indo-European, exotic as hell, vaguely mysterious and, by dint of his generous mustache and brooding eyes, he radiates just enough of that noble savage soulfulness to endear him to the middle-class masses. One more consideration: Omar Sharif is also vaguely white.

Just think, Bird, the picture would do land office business! Lobotomized Americans—particularly the discriminating movie-goers, the young set the industry caters to—they could drop into their local suburban shopping mall theater, smack down a few bucks, munch in the dark on some "buttery" popcorn and forget themselves completely for a couple of hours. Males in the audience could cuddle up into their fantasy of how, but for vagaries of happenstance, they might have been Charlie Parker, the most amazing musical virtuoso and master of improvisation since Nicolo Paganini laid down his demonic violin. But, of course, my script would play down the music and focus instead on your drug addiction, your drinking, your irresponsible ways, the debts you ran up, the fights you got into, your sex life, and all that food your could put away. Naturally, this movie would also touch on some of the other details of your colorful career, like the time you tried to do yourslf in by drinking iodine after your infant daughter Pree died.

Ah, but I tell you, man, they're still playing your stuff. Some of these kids can run your licks up and down their horns without even knowing where they came from, and would you believe that long, long ago they lifted and programmed your ideas into TV commercials and cartoon shows? Mingus called it "singing your praises while stealing your phrases." He even recorded a song about it called "Gunsling-ing Bird" which a New York poet rendered as: "If Charlie Parker Had Been a Gunslinger, There'd Be a Lot Less Rob-bins"—or something like that. While I'm on the subject of Mingus, I should tell you that he was the one who told me about how you used to call him up on the phone and lay the receiver down so he could listen to you improvise to record-ings by Stravinsky, Bartok and other European Old World composers whose techniques borrowed heavily from folk and New World sources, and from jazz in particular. That must've been something!

You were always something else, though. It was a fellow poet-novelist named Ishmael Reed who got a group of artists and business men together to create and launch a multicultu-ral arts journal in the 1970s that we christened *Yardbird Reader*. We all thought it should bear your nickname since we couldn't think of anyone else who better symbolized the quintessence of 20th Century Afro-American genius. People all over the world—especially outside this cripple-minded land where people asked if it was a magazine for convicts—loved it the way they still love your music.

Bird, I hate to tell you this, but they really are about to make *The Charlie Parker Story* out in Hollywood. You re-member Hollywood, don't you? Billy Berg's Club, the Forties, that time you practically starved and actually flipped? I was just having a little fun and putting you on a few pages back, but the honest-to-God joke is that their film is slated for pro-duction. It seems the studio couldn't or wouldn't find a Black writer knowledgeable enough to do the screenplay, but it did find a black actor to play you. He's a comedian named Ri-chard Pryor. I even wrote for him once. I know how much you loved movies, and I look forward to finding out how you're going to respond to this one. By the way, do you ever see Billie? I hope she gets to see how Diana Ross portrayed her in *Lady Sings the Blues.*

Well, I imagine you've been reuniting with some of the

old gang for quite some time. If you see Mingus, please tell him that he's missed too. But you know how it is. Nothing much has changed. Young American artists, Black musicians in particular, still have to go abroad to find recognition and audiences. I don't know what it's coming to, Bird! The Ku Klux Klan is recruiting little children now, yet what remains of the jazz tradition flourishes mainly in college and university music departments where most of the players are white.

This is simply to confirm my ever-growing respect for you and what you left the world. All I can say is thanks. Maybe that movie they're going to do will at least serve to let people in this country know what you accomplished, and that your music, which must've made somebody rich, is very much alive. There's already a statue of you in Kansas City and, I must add, a statue of the great American botanist George Washington Carver in India. What's the connection? None, except that you're both Black males of distinction in a culture where our kind is despised. But then again, Dizzy and Max did manage to get President Jimmy Carter to sing "Salt Peanuts" at a White house jazz festival some time ago, so maybe there's still some hope.

With deep affection,
AL YOUNG

one hundred years from today

SARAH VAUGHAN, 1950

Brought up on Sarah and on every other form of music that was available to me—just as surely as I was raised on grits, greens and beans—I can never forget the impact that this hushed, workaday ballad had on our rambling household. There was always something musical going on, and the wonder was that we didn't drive the neighbors crazy.

I started picking out tunes, rather accurately, on other people's pianos. I must have been halfway through my first decade. Perceiving this talent, my mother had an old upright hauled into our sparse digs in the projects on Beaubien Street in Detroit. That's when my brother Franchot, whom we now call Frank, got interested in piano and took the thing over. He was remarkable. He was so good, in fact, that my mother enrolled him for lessons with Dean Robert Nolan, a local conservatory-trained teacher who, in almost no time it seems, had Frank tossing off vibrant renditions of Debussy's "Clair de Lune," Beethoven's "Moonlight Sonata," Bach's "Gavotte," and Rimsky-Korsakov's "Flight of the Bumblebee." Frank was a prodigy who went on television, won himself a four-year scholarship to the University of Michigan's School of Music, performed with prestigious symphony orchestras, and toured the world a couple of times. At length, he was invited by President and Mrs. Johnson to perform at the White House, an honor that he and the family still cherish. Frank, however, was shy, practically reclusive, and intensely sensitive, so that the strain and vicissitudes of pursuing a concertizing career weighed heavily on him. Following a long-term stint as a professor of music at Talladega College in Alabama, he has devoted himself entirely to freelance teaching and composing.

Franchot Young's formidable command of piano was intimidating, to say the least. My younger sister Michele and I used to sneak upstairs to the attic when Frank wasn't around and practice our little homemade stuff that was unrespectable by classical standards. Michele was taking up the violin rather halfheartedly and I was doling out precious paper route money to take trumpet lessons at the Teal Studios downtown while holding down the first tuba chair in the school band and sacrificing my Saturday mornings to rehearse with the grandiose All-City Orchestra.

My mother was a Sarah Vaughan fan in the worst way. She loved to sing and her not so secret ambition was to sing just like Sarah; so much so that she learned by heart every song, every tone, every nuance of everything Sarah recorded that came within grazing range of her ear. And she didn't just mouth the sound of those tunes; she absorbed them the way the digestive system assimilates food. Whenever Sassy or the Divine Miss Vaughan—as Sarah was variously billed—hit town, Mother would be there in a front row seat, and often she took me along with her. In fact, as a consequence of her pursuit of Sarah, I was exposed at an early age to such incomparable musical legends as Nat King Cole, Billy Eckstine, Duke Ellington (whose featured saxophone soloist Johnny Hodges once invited Mom to accompany him to Paris), Jimmy Rushing, Count Basie, Dizzy Gillespie, Charlie Parker, George Shearing, Roy Haynes, Lester Young, Stan Getz, Stan Kenton, The Five Step Brothers and untold others who came rolling through the Motor City in packaged shows that played, inevitably it seems, to packed and rip-roaring crowds. Detroit was one workingclass town that loved its music, and we were Detroiters then too, weren't we?—crazy Detroiters perhaps but Detroiters all the same.

When Sarah came out with "Perdido," the Juan Tizol tune that was long a staple in the associated Ellington book, the lyric had a line about someone losing their heart at a fiesta in Toledo, referring of course to the town in Spain. My mother and I figured Sarah was talking about nearby Toledo, Ohio. What's more, Sarah did little to dispel that misinterpretation when she performed in that area of the Midwest. I'm reminded of the Ray Charles rendering of "Making Whoopee," recorded live in California, where Ray pauses ever so slightly at the word "funny," as in "some judge who thinks he's *funny*," to elicit shrieks of delight from what I imagine to be the bisexual element in the crowd. Great performers always take command of their material, put their own unmistakable stamp on it and then deliver it in such a way as to make each individual in the audience feel like a creative collaborator.

And could Sarah Vaughan ever do that! She did it so beautifully and so movingly that I've never forgotten the tears in my mother's eyes the frst time she listened to Sarah do "Street of Dreams."

She looked up at me, clutching a Kleenex and said, "You know, she's right. 'Kings don't mean a thing.' Now, that's poetry, pure poetry—whatever poetry is or is supposed to be about. That's the genuine article."

Consider my mother; lovely and eccentric, a product of the Deep American South, seated by the household piano, the home tape recorder rolling, signaling either Frank, Michele or me to provide a little back-up while she tries out her singing voice; longing to touch upon that magic something that'll carry her out of this nasty, sassy world to the portals of the divine, to a billowy, barely tangible realm of the soul where kings don't mean a thing.

"Now, just listen at that, will you," I can still hear her saying as she settles back on the sofa or into a hard kitchen chair, wherever the music happened to be stationed. "It's true, you know. What difference is any of this going to make one hundred years from today?"

al young

Considered by many to be one of America's hidden literary trea-
sures, Al Young seems to have been around forever. Since his birth
in 1939 at Ocean Springs, Mississippi, he has traveled extensively
throughout the United States and journeyed to Canada, Mexico, the
Azores, Europe, Australia and Malaysia. He grew up in the South,
the Midwest and on the West Coast. Educated at the University of
Michigan and U.C. Berkeley to teach Spanish, he continues his life-
long study of human speech and language. Along the way, he has
been a professional musician, disk jockey, medical photographer,

railroad man, warehouseman, lab aide, clerk-typist, job interviewer, janitor, editor, publisher and screenwriter. Moreover, he has taught writing and literature at such institutions as Stanford, Foothill Community College, The Colorado College, the University of Washington and the University of California at both Santa Cruz and Berkeley. Author of numerous novels and books of poetry, his film assignments include scripts for Dick Gregory, Sidney Poitier, Bill Cosby and Richard Pryor. Work of his has been translated into Norwegian, Swedish, Italian, Japanese, Spanish, Polish, Russian, French and Chinese. Al Young is the recipient of the Joseph Henry Jackson Award, National Arts Council Awards for editing and poetry, a Wallace Stegner Fellowship, a National Endowment for the Arts Fellowship, the Pushcart Prize and a Guggenheim.

This First Edition of
BODIES & SOUL
was designed by George Mattingly
with type set by Sam Doleman,
calligraphy by Sandy Diamond,
author photograph by Lee Phillips,
& cover photograph by Kaz Tsuruta,
& was printed & bound
in the United States of America, Fall 1981.

Second Edition 1984